9/09

P9-CNB-487

THE PRETTY COMMITTEE
STRIKES BACK

Little, Brown and Company

Hachette Book Group USA
1271 Avenue of the Americas, New York, NY 10020
Visit our Web site at www.lb-teens.com

First Edition: March 2006

 Produced by Alloy Entertainment
151 West 26th Street, New York, NY 10001

ISBN 0-316-11500-2

10 9 8 7 6 5
CWO
Printed in the United States of America

For Bill, Ann, and Carrie Harrison, with love.
Thank you for your endless support. This one is for you.

The thick, breathy smell of the artificial heat that blasted from the classroom's radiators made Massie Block's head pound. And the more her nature-loving geography teacher droned on about the Earth's surface and how it determines the flow of a river, the worse her headache got. Massie closed her eyes and massaged her throbbing temples until Mr. Myner finally had the decency to change the subject and talk about something that the seventh-grade girls at Octavian Country Day School actually cared about.

"Don't forget, Friday is the last day I am accepting checks for the Presidents' Day field trip to Lake Placid." Mr. Myner rolled up the sleeves on his navy flannel lumberjack shirt and revealed his muscular, too-tanned-for-February forearms.

Everyone cheered and woo-hooed.

"I am just as thrilled as you are." Mr. Myner's warm chocolate-brown eyes flickered with pride. "This is a fantastic opportunity to learn about topography, orienteering, and survival skills in the *real* outdoors."

Massie rolled her eyes. Everyone except Mr. Myner knew this trip had nothing to do with topography or survival skills. It was all about the three days they were going

1

to spend camping in the wild with the Briarwood boys. No parents, no homework, and no Principal Burns.

Anything was possible.

Even Massie found it hard to stay calm. Inside, her stomach felt all jittery, like it had grown wings and was flying around in dizzying circles. And on top of that she was starving.

For the last four days, ever since she'd given Derrick Harrington her rhinestone *M* pin, Massie had been unable to swallow anything other than Diet Dr Pepper, Luna bars, and the occasional reduced-fat Wheat Thin. She was officially hanging out with the star goalie of the Briarwood Academy soccer team, and that idea alone made digestion very difficult.

While Mr. Myner droned on about the majestic beauty of the Adirondacks, Massie made a list called:

FIVE THINGS ABOUT MY CRUSH
THAT MAKE IT IM-POSSIBLE FOR ME TO EAT

- His ah-dorable shaggy dirty-blond hair. Love, love, love when it falls in his brown eyes.
- The way he wiggles his butt after he saves a goal in soccer. Ahhhhh-dorable!
- He's the most popular seventh grader at Briarwood. And he likes *me*.
- IM'd me on Monday and said I was the cutest girl at OCD. (Take *that*, Alicia Rivera.)
- We'll be spending three days and two nights together in Lake Placid. OMG!

Massie also loved that he called her Block and that she secretly called him Derrington—a combination of his first and last names. They sounded like a gorgeous soap opera couple or a team of notorious outlaws. It was beyond hot.

Block and Derrington.

Block and Derrington.

Block and Derrington.

She was even starting to embrace the fact that he wore shorts in the dead of winter. It was his "thing." And every famous athlete had to have a "thing," or else his fans wouldn't have anything to copy. Massie's stomach suddenly tightened at the thought of Derrington surrounded by hordes of shorts-wearing fans, because in this scenario she would be the glamour girl standing by his side. The girl every other girl wanted to be. And nothing was more ah-mazing than that.

Massie wiped her sweaty palms on the green corduroy of her Joie cargo pants, then slowly lifted her purple-Swarovski-crystal-covered cell phone out of her side pocket. She waved the phone under her desk until the sparkly rhinestones caught the attention of her BFFs, alerting them that an important text message was on the way. Alicia Rivera, Dylan Marvil, Kristen Gregory, and Claire Lyons nodded. The members of the Pretty Committee were armed and ready to receive.

MASSIE: Mandatory packing meeting Sunday @ the iPad.

3

Everyone referred to Massie's bedroom as the iPad because it was all white except for a few purple accents mixed in, purple because it was the official color of royalty.

ALICIA: Can Olivia come? She's back from 2nd nose job. She'll be on the trip.

Massie couldn't understand what Alicia saw in that bubbly blonde but responded with a nod anyway. She had no choice. Last time she'd given Alicia a hard time for liking the knockoff-scarf-wearing airhead, Alicia had walked out on the Pretty Committee. And Massie didn't want to risk losing her again.

DYLAN: Need 2 shop. I went down a few sizes since the flu.

Dylan was pinching the skin on her stomach, probably wondering if she had gained any weight since lunch. Massie rolled her eyes. There were a million things Massie wanted to write back, most of them having to do with how ahn-noying Dylan's I'm-so-fat-even-when-I'm-thin routine was, but decided to drop it. Upsetting Dylan would only drive her to eat, and then Massie would have to hear about it even more. Besides, it was nice seeing Dylan with some confidence. If anything, she was much more into shopping than usual, and there was ahb-viously nothing wrong with that.

MASSIE: Shopping sounds gr8.
CLAIRE: Iin.

Massie giggled to herself. Claire was known for her late text message responses and her misspelled words because she'd only gotten her cell phone in December. If Massie hadn't secretly given it to her for Christmas, Claire would have had to wait until she was sixteen to get one from her parents. And that was *not* an option.

MASSIE: Kristen?

The girls immediately whipped their heads around and glared at Kristen. She was tugging at the sides of her recently cut-short blond hair, willing it to grow back faster. When she noticed them staring, waiting for her response, Kristen rolled her narrow aqua-colored eyes and lowered her head. Her thumbs quickly moved across her Nokia keypad.

KRISTEN: My parents still say the $1,500 fee is too much. Won't pay. H8 them.

Kristen always had money issues, and it was a major bummer.

MASSIE: Even Claire's parents are paying. It's educational.

Claire lifted her head and shot Massie a thanks-a-lot smirk. Massie shrugged innocently and returned to her vibrating phone.

ALICIA: I'll pay 4 u.
DYLAN: Me 2.

Kristen's face lit up.

MASSIE: Me 3. What's one more time?

Massie hit send and lifted her head to nod at whatever Mr. Myner was saying, just in case he was getting suspicious. But he was too caught up in his lecture about shifting glaciers, mighty rivers, and dense pine forests to care about the only part of nature that really mattered, the birds and the bees.

KRISTEN: Forget it. I'm not going.
DYLAN: ?
ALICIA: ?
CLAIRE: /
CLAIRE: Oops. I ment ???

Massie felt a sudden wave of hunger-related nausea whoosh through her entire body. She lowered her arm into her black Prada messenger bag and quietly pinched off a piece of her half-eaten Nutz Over Chocolate Luna bar. She used her fingers to grab onto her bracelet to keep the little gold charms from clanging together. The moment the chocolate-covered rice puffs grazed her lips, her cell phone vibrated. It was Derrington. Massie immediately dropped the Luna chunk back into her bag and pulled the phone close to her face.

DERRINGTON: Placid is gonna rule, fool!

She had hoped Derrington's message would be a little more personal but still chalked it up to flirting.

MASSIE:

She wanted to respond with a clever yet cute comeback. But Mr. Myner interrupted her.

"And Miss Block, let me remind you that this field trip is also a great way to add ten percent to your grade." Mr. Myner winked at Massie. His eyes seemed to look straight into her soul. Massie discreetly dropped her cell phone back into the green side pocket of her Joie cargos.

"Why are you saying that to *me*?" She slapped her French-manicured hand against her heart and widened her amber eyes. Did the whole class really have to know she'd gotten a C on the last test?

"I'm not *just* saying it to you." His voice was smooth and calming, like a late-night DJ's. "I'm saying it to everyone in the class who got below a B on the world hunger quiz."

The A students started giggling. Kristen was among them. Massie shot her a firm stop-that look. Kristen bit her lower lip and looked toward the window.

"Not all of us *need* to learn how to survive off the land." Massie glared at Mr. Myner. "Some of us can actually afford groceries and electricity. And the ones who *can* should be tested on something relevant, like European resort towns or natural hot springs."

The C students cheered and Massie bowed her head in gratitude. She knew she would eventually face Mr. Myner's wrath, but she didn't care. Their applause made it all worth it.

But before Mr. Myner could say another word, the bell rang. The high-pitched screech of chairs sliding back across the freshly waxed floors and the snapping sound of paper getting clipped back into binders meant they were done for the day.

"So, the iPad on Sunday?" Massie reconfirmed as they raced out of class. "I think everyone should show up early. This packing list may take a while."

"Count me out." Kristen pushed past them and raced down the hall.

"Why?" Massie yelled after her.

Alicia, Dylan, and Claire looked at one another and shrugged.

Kristen stopped, her back still facing them. She didn't flinch when some girls in a hurry knocked into her with their bags and coats. She just stood there, motionless.

Massie and the rest of the Pretty Committee darted over to Kristen and stood by her side. Tears were rolling down her cheeks. A black mascara booger had formed in the corner of her right eye.

"I had no idea you guys were so sick of me borrowing money." She sniffed.

Alicia nervously twirled her thick black hair into a chignon and dabbed a bit of pink lip gloss onto her full mouth. "We're so nawt." Alicia tried to sound sincere, but her voice was flat and unconvincing.

"Just let us pay," Dylan said. "If we split it four ways then—"

Alicia cleared her throat and tilted her head toward Claire.

"I mean, if we spilt it *three* ways, we could totally afford it," Dylan corrected herself.

Claire brought her thumbnail to her teeth and bit down.

"Seriously." Massie rested her hand on the back of Kristen's hot-pink-and-white Puma track jacket. "What's the big deal?"

Kristen wiggled out from under Massie's gentle grip. "Because I don't want you to think I'm some pathetic charity case."

Massie sighed. She didn't have time for this. Not when Derrington was waiting for her to respond to his text message. Maybe a little humor would lighten Kristen's mood. "You're not *some* charity case. You're *our* charity case. And we ah-dore you."

Kristen's mouth fell open and tears started rolling down her flushed cheeks.

Alicia glared at Massie.

"What?" Massie was genuinely surprised by their reactions. "I was kidding." She grabbed Kristen's hand and held it like she was about to propose marriage. "Come on, Kris. This is going to be the best week ever. Just let us pay."

"No, thanks." Kristen dried her eyes on her polyester sleeve. "I'll raise the money myself."

"How are you going to raise fifteen hundred dollars in two days?" Claire sounded genuinely interested.

"I am going to teach memory skills," Kristen said.

"What?" the girls said together.

"I am taking a home course in photographic memory skills, and it's really working," Kristen explained.

"Okay, so what did we read about in geo today? Word for word?" Dylan pulled up her new size-two denim miniskirt, then checked to see if anyone noticed.

Massie quickly looked away.

Kristen cocked her head, ran her fingers through her short blond hair, and smiled. "We didn't read anything today. Mr. Myner spent the whole class talking about stupid Lake Placid."

"Hmmm." Dylan tapped her index finger against her pursed lips. "Not bad."

"Why tutor when we can just give you the money?" Massie asked.

"I'll be fine," Kristen insisted. "I have five hundred dollars in my savings account, so all I need is a thousand dollars."

Massie smiled. "Maybe you could teach math, too."

Kristen giggled, then wiped away her last tear. "I'm serious. If I charge ten girls a hundred dollars each, I'll be able to go."

"Great. Now can we please go shopping for earth tones?" Dylan whined.

"Yes." Alicia bounced up and down on her toes. "I'm desperate." She tightened the knot on her short ballet-pink tie-front cardigan and her cleavage practically tripled.

"Oh good, I need some new underwear." Claire's blue eyes widened with excitement. "Can we go to Victoria's Secret?"

"Given," Alicia agreed. "I need a new br—" She crossed her arms over her C-cups. "I need some things too."

The girls started walking toward the exit to meet Isaac, Massie's driver. He'd warned them that he might be late because a new fridge was getting installed in the backseat of the Range Rover. "See you guys." Kristen waved. Her voice was full of purpose and determination.

"Aren't you coming?" Massie asked.

"Nah, I'm going to use the Xerox machine to make flyers for my course," Kristen said.

"Want help?" Massie pushed open the wood doors and stepped into the cold.

"Yeah, I'd love some." Kristen's face lit up. "Wanna come with me to make my posters?"

Massie felt her stomach lurch. She hadn't actually expected Kristen to say yes.

"Uh, I can't because Isaac is on his way," Massie shouted. "Good luck. Call me later."

"Uh, thanks." Kristen turned toward the library.

"Good luck," the others echoed as they followed Massie outside.

"Think she'll be able to raise a thousand dollars by Friday?" Dylan pulled a hunter green knit cap out of her turquoise Marc Jacobs duffel and forced it over her mass of red curls.

"Only if your famous mother turns her morning talk show into a telethon," Alicia said. Dylan's mom, Merri-Lee Marvil, was the host of a super-popular morning show, *The Daily Grind*.

"That would be so cool." Claire zipped up her baby blue Old Navy puffy coat. "Do you think she could get Joss Stone?"

"She can get *anyone*." Dylan smiled proudly. "And I bet she could raise the money in like five minutes."

"Gawd, where's Isaac?" Massie stood on her toes and looked out into the empty parking lot. She would have said anything to change the subject. Kristen's whole poverty thing was a major snoozer. And Dylan's famous mother was running a close second. The only thing that held Massie's interest these days was Derrington.

A white Lexus and two black Audis pulled into the lot. Livvy Collins, Alexandra Regan, and Carrie Randolph waved to the drivers as they strolled down the school steps, taking their time so they could finish their conversation.

"I *know* Nina was a total fake." Alexandra buttoned up her winter white Banana Republic boiled wool coat. "But how great would it be to have her on this Lake Placid trip?"

"Totallyagreed," slurred Carrie, the notorious fast talker. "Nooneknewmoreaboutguys."

Suddenly Massie felt dizzy. It was one thing to hear her classmates idolize Nina Callas—Alicia's Spanish slutbag of a cousin, who was responsible for almost tearing Massie and Derrington apart—but it was quite another for them to consider her an *expert* in anything other than lying, stealing, and cheesy Euro style. Besides, Massie had assumed that when Nina returned to Spain, things would go back to normal and she would become the all-around expert again. So why wasn't that happening? She lowered herself onto the stone steps. Alicia, Dylan, and Claire sat down beside her.

"Maybe we could get her e-mail address from Alicia." Livvy bit down on her plump bottom lip, chewing off her clear lip gloss. "I bet she could give us some killer tips."

"Lovethat." Carrie clapped her lambskin mittens together. "Hey, look, theresheis!"

"Nina?" Livvy and Alexandra shrieked at the same time.

"No, A-*licia*." Carrie stomped her foot. She pulled her friends by their coats and dragged them down the steps.

The well-coiffed woman inside the white Lexus honked the horn.

"Holdonaminutemah." Carrie stomped her foot again and held up her index finger.

The two black Audis beeped next. Alexandra and Livvy held up their fingers the same way Carrie had.

"What?" Massie rose to her feet. Alicia, Claire, and Dylan immediately joined her side.

"We actually wanted to ask Alicia something." Carrie seemed to be speaking to Massie's burnt orange suede Michael Kors nonwaterproof snow boots.

"Well, if it has to do with her trashy cousin Nina, don't bother," Massie hissed. "She's dead to us."

"We just want her e-mail address." Livvy stepped in. The blond ballet dancer–slash–basketball player was the thinnest and tallest one in the group, but Massie refused to look up at her. Instead, she spoke to the scratched rhinestone buttons on her tacky wannabe antique coat.

Dylan burst out laughing. "Stupid much? Like they have e-mail in Spain!"

Claire and Alicia giggled at Dylan's ignorance but Massie shot them a look, warning them to stop.

Carrie, Alexandra, and Livvy seemed to believe Dylan, because they all turned red and looked away. It was the perfect time for Massie to pounce.

"Look, I know the only reason you would want to speak to that slut-o-rita is to get guy advice before the trip." Massie softened her voice so she'd sound sweet and caring. The girls lifted their heads, and Massie stepped down and joined them on their level. "Am I right?"

"Yeah." Livvy scraped more lip gloss into her mouth.

"I totally understand." Massie patted Livvy's shoulder. "That's why I'm offering a secret kissing clinic before the trip." She waved her hand behind her back so Claire, Dylan, and Alicia wouldn't question her.

One of the black Audis honked again.

"ONE MINUTE, MAH," Alexandra shouted. Then she leaned in toward Massie and whispered, "What's kissing like? Tell me *everything*. Don't leave one thing out."

"It's hard to describe." Massie spoke louder than she needed to. "Derrington and I have been making out for a while now—since the holidays, to be exact." She elbowed Alexandra in the rib and winked. "Thank Gawd for mistletoe, if you know what I mean!"

Claire cracked up. Massie waved her hand again.

"Who do you think taught Nina how to kiss?" Claire chimed in. Massie was grateful for the backup.

"What?" Alicia screeched.

"Is that true?" Massie heard Dylan whisper.

Massie stepped in front of her friends, blocking them from the conversation.

"I have a few spaces left in my kissing clinic if you want to sign up," Massie offered. "But you can't tell a soul. I've already had to turn a lot of people away, and it wouldn't be fair."

"Wewon'ttell." Carrie squinted and shook her head, her saucer-shaped brown eyes barely open.

"Swear." Livvy made an invisible cross on her tacky coat to prove her sincerity.

"Double swear." Alexandra crossed her boiled wool twice. "This is gonna be so great." Her smile revealed a mouthful of emerald green braces.

"'Kay, we're meeting in the OCD Serenity Chapel Friday after school." Massie's tone was hushed and secretive.

"Okay," Livvy whispered back. "But are we actually gonna have to kiss someone?"

"Ignore her." Alexandra giggled. "She's a little bit of a wuss. But *I* can't wait."

The horns honked again.

"Coming." Alexandra ran down the steps toward her impatient mother, and the other girls followed.

"I am *not* a wuss," Livvy insisted to no one in particular.

"Thanks, Massie," Carrie shouted. "Iwon'ttellanyone."

"Shhhh." Alexandra put her finger to her lips. "It's a secret, remember?"

"Ooops." Carrie laughed. "Sorry."

"Oh, don't forget the fee," Massie yelled after them. All three girls stopped in front of their mothers' cars and looked back at Massie. "Twenty bucks a person. Cash only."

The girls smiled back and waved goodbye.

"Are you actually going to take their money?" Claire asked Massie as the girls pulled away.

"Of course." Massie half smiled. "I'll donate it to Kristen's Lake Placid fund."

"Nice." Claire gave Massie a thumbs-up. "But do you think she'll take it?"

"I'll tell her I want to hire her to tape the clinic—you know, so I can put it on my new video blog," Massie said.

"When did you start a video blog?" Dylan asked.

"And when did you become a kissing expert?" Alicia added.

Massie looked at Claire, silently begging her for help.

"Over the holidays." Claire vouched for her friend. "I thought everyone knew that."

Massie shook her head. "I don't like to kiss and tell."

"Ooops, sorry." Claire hit herself on the head, like she should have known better.

Massie was pleased with her friend's willingness to play along. Claire was the only one who knew the truth about Massie's lack of experience with boys and was smart enough to know that Massie wanted to keep it a secret.

"It's okay." Massie continued her Oscar-worthy performance. "But if you must know, Derrington and I have been getting pretty busy these days."

"No way!" Alicia slapped Massie's arm.

"It's true." Claire jumped in. "I walked in on them back when Massie and I were sharing a bedroom. They were in a full-on lip lock."

Massie shrugged and looked away, brushing her cheek against her shoulder as she turned. She wanted to look sweet in spite of her new racy reputation.

"Can we take your clinic too?" Alicia asked. "I played spin-the-bottle a few times in Spain, but those kisses were closed-mouthed. And I'm so beyond ready to go open."

"Really?" Dylan teased. "With who?"

"Josh Hotz." Alicia rolled her eyes. "Given!"

Dylan giggled, knowing full well that Alicia had had a crush on the preppy, Polo-loving Briarwood boy for weeks. But Massie, who knew the rest of the story, casually glanced at Claire, who was biting her pinky nail.

If Alicia knew Claire had already kissed Josh, she would send her back to Orlando in last year's Louis Vuitton Cerises bag. And it was obvious from Claire's nervous expression that she was well aware of this.

"What about you and Cam?" Alicia asked Claire. "Have you kissed yet?"

"Uh, not yet." Claire's fair complexion turned scarlet. "Any day now. Hopefully the clinic will help me get some confidence."

Massie looked out at the emptying parking lot, knowing how hard it must have been for Claire to sound chipper when she talked about Cam. Because the truth was, ever since last weekend, when Cam had seen Claire and Josh kissing after the Briarwood soccer finals, he had wanted nothing to do with her. He wouldn't even give Claire a chance to explain. If he had, he'd have found out that Nina had purposely made it seem like Cam liked *her*, not Claire. And once he understood *that*, he'd get why Claire was so hurt, and he'd have to forgive her for kissing Josh. But for now, Massie was the only one who knew any of this.

"I wanna kiss Chris Plovert," Dylan declared. "I'm a sucker for a wounded boy on crutches."

"I thought you stopped liking him after the Love Struck dance," Alicia said.

"I did, but now that I'm a size two, I have no goals." Dylan pulled off her green hat and fluffed her hair. "My life seems boring and pointless. I need a good make-out to spice things up."

"Great, so you're all in?" Massie asked as her family's silver Range Rover pulled into the parking lot, headlights flashing.

"In," Alicia confirmed.

"In," Dylan agreed.

"In," Claire added.

Massie stepped down off the cement curb expecting Isaac, her driver, to step out of the SUV and open the door for her. Instead her mother, Kendra, rolled down the window and smiled. Some breathy Norah Jones song was playing at full blast.

"Guess who?" Kendra shouted above the music.

"Mom?" Massie sounded like she hadn't seen the woman in years. "What are you doing here?"

Kendra smoothed her freshly manicured hands over her brown chin-length bob and tried to act shocked. But her recent round of Botox injections made her look more stunned than surprised. "Since when is it strange for a mother to pick up her daughter from school?"

"Since third grade," Massie responded. "When we got Isaac."

"Well, he lost a filling and had to run to Dr. Wilson, and

Inez was in the middle of making her scallop linguini so I thought it would be fun to—"

"You know we drive Alicia and Dylan home, right?" Massie asked.

"I do now." Kendra popped the automatic locks on the door so the girls could get in. "All aboard."

Massie slid across the buttery soft backseat with her friends, like she always did, leaving Kendra up front alone. She leaned forward. "Mom, we were going to go to the mall. You know, to get stuff for our trip."

"Sounds good to me." Kendra stepped on the gas and the car jerked forward. She slammed on the brakes and the girls fell on top of each other and broke into fits of laughter.

"Seat belts, everyone," Kendra shouted over her shoulder.

No one argued.

Once they were on the road, the girls started talking about what stores to hit first. But Massie had other things on her mind, like how she was going to teach a clinic on making out when the only guy she had ever kissed was her father. And a quick peck on the cheek was hardly what her friends had in mind. That much she definitely knew.

"Your room is a total ten." Layne Abeley flopped down on Claire's new bed and bounced a few times, like she was testing the coils and springs in the mattress. She ran her black-painted fingernails over the glittery stars on the sky blue down comforter and slowly shook her head. "Unbelievably cool."

"I know, I love it." Claire's insides filled up with so much pride, she thought she'd pop, like one of the annoying watermelon Bubble Yum bubbles Layne was blowing.

Claire pulled off her socks and padded across her fluffy white sheepskin rug. "Can you believe the Blocks paid for all of it?" She reached inside the decorative lemon yellow locker that held her CD collection and reached for her favorite mix, *Cam's Christmas Carlos*. Claire used to giggle when she saw how he'd accidentally misspelled *carols*. It made her feel close to him. But tonight, when she fed the mix to her new Bose sound system, her insides felt like they were getting sucked out of her belly button. She felt hollow and empty without Cam in her life.

"Actually I *can* believe they paid for it." Layne's green eyes widened and filled with horror as "All I Want for Christmas Is You" blasted through the four white speakers

21

that hung from the corners of Claire's ceiling. "What I can't believe is that they finally let you toss Massie's dead grandmother's old furniture and get new stuff. I felt like I stepped out of a time machine every time I came over. It took days to get the smell of mothballs out of my hair."

Claire chuckled and was suddenly overcome by a rush of warm appreciation for Layne, her special friend: the one she could let her guard down with, shop at Target with, eat sugar and fat with. Layne was not part of the Pretty Committee and probably never would be, and that was more than fine with Claire. It was nice having a friend who saw Westchester the same way she did, through the eyes of a coat-check girl at a black-tie affair.

Claire's emotions had been up and down like this for days. Whenever she thought about Cam, every bone in her body felt like it had been stuffed with lead. She'd sigh a lot and stare off into the distance, wondering if she'd ever be able to smile again. Then, minutes later, she'd share a moment of true friendship with Layne or Massie and her teeth would start chattering with joy. But one thing had been for sure: both the highs and the lows usually ended in tears.

"Why are we listening to Christmas music in February?" Layne pulled a pair of bile yellow Converse sneakers out of her Sunshine Tours bag. She dumped a Ziploc bag of black rhinestones on Claire's bed and reached for the glue gun she'd "borrowed" from art class.

"Cam burned this for me." Claire curled up in a ball on

a stack of pillows on the floor by the window. Inez, the Blocks' live-in housekeeper, had made them from Claire's old T-shirts from Orlando. It was either that or Massie was going to use them to pull poo-berries off her dog Bean's butt, and Claire had given in. She had lived in Westchester for six months, which was long enough to know that the "right time" to wear an oversize Lisa Simpson tee would never, ever present itself.

"I should have known Cam was behind this cheddar-filled mix." Layne smeared glue all over the rubbery tops of her sneakers. She pinched a rhinestone and dropped it on the sticky surface. Then she slowly dragged it into position and reached for another one. "Are you going to do your new Keds?" Layne waved a Ziploc full of pink rhinestones in Claire's direction.

Claire shrugged and curled up into a tight ball. The sound of Layne slurping forced her to lift her head.

"What's with you and those Go-Gurts? They're gross." The thought of gooey liquid yogurt in a tube made Claire's insides churn almost as much as they did when she thought about Cam.

Layne spit a wad of Bubble Yum into the empty tube and tossed it into Claire's blue glass trash can. "Why so cranky?" Layne asked during a long wet burp.

"Ewww." Claire buried her face again and wondered why she hadn't told Layne what had happened between her and Cam. She imagined herself saying, "Hey Layne, guess what? Last weekend Cam dumped me." And immediately had her answer. Speaking those words out loud would make them true and Claire wasn't ready to accept that. Massie was the only one who knew the truth. And that was because she'd had a hot tip from Derrington and possessed a knack for interrogation.

"Come sit next to me so we can finish these sneakers before Lake Placid." Layne dropped three black rhinestones onto her shoe at once. Two of them fell facedown.

"Ugh." She used her long pinky nail to flip them back over.

Claire put her Simpsons Orlan-d'oh! pillow on her lap and ran her fingers along the soft cotton. Her favorite sleeping shirt had been reduced to a decorative accent. What had once given her tremendous comfort was now just a memory. Just like Cam.

"You should put a rhinestone *C* on each one of your shoes," Layne suggested. "You know, one for *Claire* and one for *Cam*."

"We're done," Claire blurted out.

Layne lifted her head. "Why?" She ran her fingers through her teased brown hair. "Is it because I'm using glue on your new bedspread?"

"Huh?" Claire crinkled her pale eyebrows. Then she shook her head and exhaled sharply though her button nose. "No, I mean me and Cam. We're done. He dumped me." The sound of those words coming out of her own mouth brought a swell of tears to her eyes.

"What?" Layne jumped off the bed. She crouched beside

the nest of T-shirt pillows, unbuttoned her tight pink cords, then let herself drop to the floor. "What happened?"

Claire wanted to tell Layne the truth, but what if she didn't understand? Or worse, what if she sided with Cam?

"He said he lost interest," Claire murmured to her cuticles. "He didn't want to be tied down."

"Cam *Fisher* said that?" Layne asked. "About *you*?"

Claire nodded. At that moment, it was physically impossible for her to look Layne in the eye.

"Did you check for hidden cameras?" Layne asked sincerely. "Maybe you were on some prank show. I mean, there's no way Cam would—"

"He did, okay?" Claire snapped.

A heavy, uncomfortable silence hung over their heads like one of Mr. Block's giant striped golf umbrellas.

"I've got it." Layne jumped to her feet, refastened her cords, and lifted her index finger in the air. She started pacing back and forth.

"Maybe he misses the old you." Her green eyes flickered. "You know, the girl he first fell in love with."

"Huh?" Claire wished she had the guts to tell Layne the truth.

"We have to get you back to the old Claire. The one Cam first noticed."

"What old Claire?"

"Claire B.P.C." Layne said with a proud smile, like she had just said something brilliantly clever. Claire stared at her blankly.

"Before the Pretty Committee!" Layne wheeled Claire's industrial-looking full-length mirror across the room. "See for yourself."

Claire pushed herself up and stood in front of the mirror with her hands on her narrow waist.

"You've lost your Florida charm. Your cute Disney bangs have grown out, you traded in your cherry ChapStick for lip gloss, and you wear boot-cut jeans instead of overalls," Layne said. "You're not the girl Cam first fell in love with."

Even though Claire knew the real reason Cam had dumped her, she couldn't help but wonder if Layne had a point.

"Maybe you should cut bangs again," Layne said. "I bet once Cam saw the old Claire, he'd want you back."

Claire knew this was ridiculous, but like any desperate person, she felt compelled to take a leap of faith and give it a try. Who knew, it just might be the thing that worked.

"Fine." Claire sighed. "Maybe I'll ask Massie to call Jakkob for an appointment."

Layne stopped pacing, put her hands on her chunky hips, and shook her head. "You just don't get it, do you?"

"Get what?" Claire felt a wave of prickly heat under her arms. She hated being left out of an inside joke, especially when it was at her own expense.

"Ugh." Layne lifted her hands in frustration. "Claire B.P.C. would not call Ja-kkkkkkkob for a cut."

"She wouldn't?"

"No, she'd do it herself."

Layne stomped over to the bed, grabbed her Sunshine Tours bag, and dumped it upside down. Chewed pencils, three quarters, two dimes, six pennies, one Susan B. Anthony dollar, red hair elastics, two bottles of nail polish— one black, one fluorescent yellow—liquid eyeliner, two tubes of vanilla Go-Gurt, Carmex, Kleenex, a mini pink calculator, a Hello Kitty money clip filled with Big Red gum, three loose house keys, a disposable digital camera, a rolled up Delia's catalogue, and a baby blue Miss Army pocket knife spilled onto the freshly bleached hardwood floor.

Layne reached for the Miss Army knife and unhinged a few of its hidden tools: a nail file, a mirror, and a pair of tweezers. "Where are those cute little scissors?"

"You're so not cutting my hair with that Swiss Army knife thing." Claire jumped to her feet.

"Got 'em." Layne unfolded the collapsible scissors and forced her fingers into the tiny holes. "They're a little stiff, but they'll do the trick."

"No way." Claire darted for her bedroom door, grabbed her red bike helmet off the hook, slammed it on her head, and tightened the chin strap. "Let's see if those tiny scissors can get through *this*." Claire knocked on the metallic plastic and giggled. Her mood suddenly shifted again and she felt light and giddy. She almost felt like Claire B.C.E.—Before Cam Ended.

"No problem." Layne scraped her foot along the floor three times, like a charging bull, and ran headfirst into Claire's stomach.

"Get off of me." Claire was laughing so hard it sounded like "Offa eeee."

Layne tackled Claire, throwing her onto the bed. She climbed on top of her and pinned her down by kneeling on her thin arms. Claire squirmed and bucked. But Layne held firm.

"Stop moving or I'll Go-Gurt fart on you."

"Ew, get off!" Claire laughed and bucked even harder. Her hair was starting to sweat under the helmet and her scalp was getting itchy.

"Is everything all right in there?" Judi Lyons knocked on her daughter's bedroom door, then opened it just enough to stick the tip of her button nose inside the room.

"Yeah, we're fine, Mom," Claire panted.

"Hi, Mrs. Lyons." Layne's voice was sweet and innocent. "Sorry for the noise." She dug her knees deeper into Claire's arms.

"No problem," Judi replied kindly. "Have fun." She backed away from the door but left it open a crack.

As soon as her mother left, Claire started bucking again.

"If you lie perfectly still, I'll get up." Layne's body was being flung from side to side.

"Fine," Claire panted.

"Stayyy." Layne held her index finger in between Claire's eyes like she was training a dog. "Stayyyy," she said again.

Before Claire could stop her, Layne whipped the scissors out from behind her back and in one smooth motion snipped the chin strap on Claire's helmet. Claire lifted her head in shock and the helmet slipped right off. Layne rolled off Claire and onto the floor. She kicked her legs in the air and pumped her arms over her head. "Victory!" she shouted.

"You ruined my bike helmet," Claire shouted, trying as hard as she could to suppress the smile that was forcing itself across her flushed cheeks.

"You're welcome," Layne said. "If Cam ever saw you in that thing, it would be over for good."

Claire felt the lead returning to her bones. Her smile started to fade.

"Now, let's work on those bangs." Layne grabbed Claire's arm and pulled her over to the full-length mirror by the window.

Claire allowed herself to be led. "I dunno. It took me four months to grow these out."

"Your call." Layne cut the air with the tiny scissors. They were so stiff they squeaked.

Claire sighed. "Okay, why not?" She had a feeling she'd regret it, but at least she'd have something else to worry about besides Cam.

"Cool." Layne rested her hands on Claire's shoulders and turned her around to face the mirror.

"Don't you want me to face you?" Claire asked.

"No. This is how they do it at the hairdresser's."

"Fine, do it."

Layne reached into the back pocket of her dusty pink cords and pulled out a peppermint Altoid. She popped it in her mouth and stood right in Claire's face. Layne's butt was reflected in the mirror and Claire checked to see if there was a metal Altoids tin imprint on her back pocket. There wasn't. The mint had been in there naked, probably all hot and soft from Layne sitting on it all day. Claire shook her head.

Layne quickly moved the scissors away from Claire's forehead. "Don't move."

"Sorry." Claire rolled her eyes. But she was glad Layne was taking this seriously.

The tiny scissors came toward Claire's face and for some reason the *Jaws* music started playing in her head: *Da-na da-na da-na . . .*

Layne pinched a clump of hair between her two fingers and Claire squeezed her eyes shut. The scissors squeaked once and a flurry of yellow hair fell to the floor.

"Let me see." Claire moved her head to the side so she could look in the mirror, but Layne grabbed her chin and held it in place.

"Don't move or you'll mess up my line." A cool mint smell rushed out of Layne's mouth. "You can look when I'm done."

Claire took a deep breath, shut her eyes again, and waited for the next squeak. "I'm so good," Layne said to Claire's bangs. "This looks perfect."

Claire felt her shoulders relax. Having her old bangs back might be fun.

"One more snip and you're done," Layne said with a satisfied sigh.

She pinched the last bit of hair and slid the scissors into position.

"AIBO! COME 'ERE, AIBO!" Todd, Claire's ten-year-old brother, shouted in the hallway.

The sudden noise startled Layne and she released Claire's hair.

Both girls let out a sigh of relief.

"That was close." Layne sighed. "Good thing I wasn't midcut."

"Sorry. Aibo is Todd's new robot dog. He's in love with it."

"A robot dog?"

"Yeah. He wants a real one but my parents don't think he's responsible enough, so they're making him prove himself with this stupid barking robot."

Layne bit down on her Altoid and reached for Claire's hair again. First the pinch, then the squeak, and then Todd kicked open Claire's bedroom door with the heel of his L. L. Bean boots.

Layne screamed and jumped, just as the scissors bit down on Claire's hair.

"Have you seen Aibo?" Todd shouted.

"NO!" Claire wailed.

"Nice hair," said the freckly redhead. He chuckled into his hand and slammed the door behind him.

Claire pushed Layne aside and looked in the mirror.

Most of her bangs were perfect . . . except for the part above her nose, which was two inches shorter and crooked. Claire immediately flashed back to the third grade when her front teeth were missing and she spoke with a lisp. She'd wanted to cry every time someone asked her what her last name was, because it came out sounding like *Lyonth*. Eventually she'd dropped the *s* and referred to herself simply as Claire Lyon until her big teeth grew in.

"I can't believe this." Claire's ears started ringing and her vision became narrow and a little blurry around the edges. "It looks like I got a haircut in the Leaning Tower of Pisa." She thought of the hair clips, the gels, the endless tugging and training that had gone into getting her blond bangs to finally reach behind her ears. Now, one mistake and they were gone. Just like that.

Just like Cam.

Layne knelt down on the floor and quietly started putting her things back in the Sunshine Tours bag.

All Claire could do was stare at her crooked bangs and wonder who she wanted to kill more, Todd, Layne, or herself.

The ding of an IM lifted Claire out of her daze. She hurried toward her gray Dell computer. Was Cam finally ready to forgive her?

"Is it him?" Layne jumped to her feet and joined Claire. "I knew the bangs would work."

"It's only Massie," Claire moped.

"*Only* Massie," Layne teased.

They both knew six months ago a friendly IM from Massie Block would have made Claire's life. That fact wasn't lost on Claire; she was just too depressed to acknowledge it.

MASSIEKUR: U CAN'T EVER LET ALICIA KNOW U KISSED JOSH HOTZ. WE'RE ON THE PHONE NOW. SHE'S BEEN TALKING BOUT HIM 4 LAST HOUR.

Claire immediately positioned herself between Layne and the screen. But it was too late. She could feel the heat of Layne's minty breath on the back of her neck while she typed her reply message.

CLAIREBEAR: CALL U L8TR. TALKING 2 MOM.

Claire hit send and turned off her computer. "So, what time do you have to be home?" She avoided Layne by straitening up the mussed comforter on her bed.

"You kissed Josh Hotz?" Layne dove onto the comforter and rolled around until she had undone all of Claire's tidying. "Why didn't you tell me? When did you become such a big slutburger with everything on it?"

"That's why." Claire bit down on her thumbnail.

"I'm kidding, I don't think you're a slutburger. I used to make out with Eli all the time in his laundry room."

"You did?" Claire finally looked at her friend. "Why didn't you tell me?"

"I didn't want you to call me a slutburger," Layne said.

Claire wanted to laugh, but all she could manage was a weak smile.

"Does Cam know?" Layne asked.

Claire plopped down on her bed and shrugged. She ran her fingers along the clear stitching on her comforter, willing herself not to cry.

"Wait, is *that* why Cam dumped you?" Layne slapped the bed.

Claire shrugged again.

"Come on, tell me. I hate that Massie Block knows more about your life than I do."

Claire tried to smile again but couldn't.

"Pleeeease." Layne clapped her hands. "I'll tell you something totally embarrassing about me."

"Only if you promise not to think I'm lame." Claire lifted her head.

"Promise." Layne held her palm in the air and crossed her heart.

"Fine." Claire leaned in toward Layne just in case her eavesdropping brother and his fake dog were listening at the door. Then, in a hushed tone, she told Layne how Nina had made it look like Cam was over Claire and how that had driven her into the arms of another boy.

"So Josh told Cam you kissed him?" Layne unwrapped a

stick of Big Red gum and stuffed it in her mouth. "What a loser."

"No." Claire shook her head slowly. "Cam saw us."

"Brutal!" Layne shoved another piece of gum in her mouth. "But it served him right for ignoring you, right?"

"I dunno." Claire lowered her head. "Turns out it wasn't really his fault."

"How?"

"Later I found out Nina told Cam she'd put a Spanish soccer spell on him, that if he ignored me, their team would win the finals. She told him I knew about it, so he didn't think I'd be upset."

"Didn't they lose that game?"

Claire nodded.

"So after the game, when Cam realized the whole spell thing was bogus, he came to talk to me, and that's when he saw . . ." Claire's voice trailed off.

"Why don't you just explain what happened." Layne chomped on her gum.

"I tried." Claire smoothed the foil on one of Layne's discarded wrappers. "He won't take my calls or read my e-mails. Nothing works."

"Wow, he actually fell for that Spanish soccer spell thing?"

"I guess people will believe anything when they're desperate." Claire tugged on her short bangs.

"Maybe you should write him a poem," Layne suggested. "Those usually work."

"You think?"

"Totally." Layne nodded once. "I sent one to my dad when I wanted a bike and the next week there was a brand-new Bratz Beauty bike in my driveway."

"Wasn't that a surprise for your next-door neighbor?" Claire asked.

"Yeah, but when I told my dad I wanted one just like it, he promised to get me one for my birthday."

"And you think that's because of the poem you wrote him?"

"It didn't hurt. Besides, Cam is a total softy. He's always burning CDs for you and bringing you candy. He's such a poem guy."

"Hmmm." Claire was reluctant to take any more of Layne's advice, but she did have a point. Cam was a total romantic. He was probably waiting for Claire to make an effort, something more than an e-mail or a text message. "Maybe I'll try it."

"You should." Layne stood up and put on her white pleather trench coat. "I better go. Dinner is early tonight because my parents are on some new diet where they can't eat past six-thirty p.m."

"Wait." Claire stood up and ran toward her door. She leaned against it until it closed, then stayed there, blocking Layne. "What's your embarrassing secret?"

Layne tightened the belt on her coat and threw her Sunshine Tours bag over her shoulder. "Oh, that. It's no big deal. I'll tell you tomorrow."

"No way." Claire pushed Layne away from the door. "You promised."

"Fine." Layne rolled her green eyes. "If you must know, I got my period last month."

"No way!" Claire didn't know anyone who'd had her period yet.

"Yeah way!" Layne said. "And I'm terrified I'll get it again when we're in Lake Placid."

"What's it like?"

"It's like what your nose is going to look like if you tell anyone." Layne stepped toward the door.

"I won't," Claire promised.

"Look, I have to go." Layne's face was bright red. "I'll call you later."

Claire stepped aside and let her friend leave. She was ready to spend some alone time in front of the mirror anyway, just her and her short, crooked bangs.

A rush of panic shot through Claire's body when she saw the damage up close. It had taken her four months to grow out her bangs, and now they were even worse than they had been before. How would she face the Pretty Committee?

She had been right about one thing: the ridiculous haircut was taking her mind off of Cam.

Claire took a deep breath, reached into the back of her closet, and pulled out her old wood box of hair clips. It had been months since she'd needed them. She took out the silver seashell barrette, the one she'd first worn when she arrived in Westchester, and fastened her lopsided bangs to the side of her head. Then she took a deep breath and powered up her computer. At the top of the page she typed, *Miss Understood*. After that the words flowed out of her like tears.

> MISS UNDERSTOOD
> by Claire Lyons
>
> You used to send me e-mails
> And gummy worms galore.
> I stopped biting my nails
> Because I wasn't lonely anymore.
>
> I'd stare into your eyes,
> One green and one blue;
> We'd share a plate of fries
> And I'd dream of kissing you.
>
> But Cam, you broke my heart like glass,
> And all because of Nina Call-as.
> You acted like we were through,
> And so J.H. I had to choose.
>
> I never liked him as more than a friend;
> I was hurt because I got dissed.
> Please don't say that this is the end:
> I won't be happy till we've kissed.

And without reading it over, Claire hit send. Because that's what desperate people do.

If Massie had known she'd be crouching in the balcony of the Serenity Chapel, spying on Dylan and Alicia after school, she never would have worn her denim Chip & Pepper miniskirt.

If they'd happened to look up, they would have caught their newly appointed kissing guru squatting like a frog, making little effort to conceal her turquoise Cosabella thong underwear.

Massie prayed to Gawd that Principal Burns would burst through the heavy oak doors and bust her friends for sneaking into the forbidden chapel after school. That was plan A and her only way out. If the girls got caught, they'd immediately get kicked out of the chapel and sent home for the rest of the day. Then the kissing lesson would be canceled and Massie would have more time to build up the courage to truly kiss Derrington and get some real experience. Because now all she had to share with her disciples were a few makeshift props and a big load of crap.

Livvy Collins, Alexandra Regan, and Carrie Randolph tiptoed across the royal blue carpet and disappeared into the choir pit below the pulpit where Dylan and Alicia were hiding. The sounds of giggling followed by loud *shhhh*'s rose up to the balcony every time another girl stepped down into the pit, filling Massie with nervous desperation. She had deployed hundreds of insane tactics to maintain her queen bee status, but this one was the most ridiculous. Not only was she claiming to be an expert on something she knew nothing about, she was flat-out lying to Kristen, Alicia, and Dylan. And that took social warfare to new heights.

Massie would give Principal Burns five more minutes to shut down the party and if she didn't, Massie would have to give her public what they'd come for.

Claire and her ahn-noying activist friend Layne came in next. They weren't giddy like the other girls. They weren't whispering or giggling. Instead, Claire was chewing her thumbnail and Layne was shaking her head back and forth like she was way too mature to be there. For a split second, Massie wondered if Claire had told Layne the truth; that the kissing clinic was a ploy for Massie to get her credibility back after Nina had hijacked it. But she immediately shook the idea from her head. Claire knew better than to betray Massie's confidence. Besides, Massie knew Claire's secret about kissing Josh Hotz. All she had to do was leak that to Alicia and Claire would be reduced to LBR (loser beyond repair) status all over again. Alicia would make sure of it.

Massie inched a little closer to the edge of the balcony to see if Claire's bangs had been able to work through some of their problems since lunch, but no such luck. They were still short and crooked. Jakkob would have to be notified over the weekend. The newest member of the Pretty

Committee could *not* go on the Lake Placid trip looking like the Bride of Chucky. It would reflect poorly on all of them.

Kristen shuffled in a few steps behind Claire and Layne, carrying the Sony mini DV camera that she'd checked out of the A/V department. She was ready to capture the lesson for Massie's new video blog. Massie searched the chapel, her amber eyes shifting from one stained-glass window to the next, hoping Gawd might appear and save her.

"Helll-oooo," shouted someone from the back of the chapel. Massie couldn't see who it was because the balcony hung past the entrance and blocked her view.

"Al-eeee-SHA, are you in here?"

A loud *shhhh!* resounded from the choir pit.

"We're in here," Alicia whisper-shouted.

"Oh," yelled the girl. "I thought I missed the kissing—"

Another group *shhhh* cut her off.

"Sorry." She snickered and hurried to join the others.

It wasn't Gawd after all. It was Olivia Ryan, one of His biggest mistakes.

Olivia was like Alicia's dumb puppy dog everyone happened to think was cute. But Massie couldn't stand Olivia and had a hard time understanding what Alicia saw in her. Granted, she was undeniably pretty in a different way than Alicia was.

Olivia was perky and all-American, with her wavy blond hair, her navy blue eyes, and cute ski-slope nose—courtesy of Dr. Marriott— while Alicia was more of a sultry exotic beauty. And together they were ah-nnoyingly hot. The seventh-grade

Briarwood boys referred to them as the Twenty, since they were both tens. Massie hated that nickname almost as much as she hated not being included in it. Would changing their name to the Thirty be so inconceivable?

Once Olivia disappeared into the pit, Massie took a deep breath and exhaled slowly. She reviewed her notes and exhaled again. It was time.

Massie heard the bones behind her knees crack when she finally stood up. Her legs felt stiff and sore from crouching. She adjusted her skirt and added a fresh coat of MAC gloss to her lips, even though she could still feel the weight of the sticky layer she had applied when she'd first gotten there. She cleared her throat, touched the crown charm on her bracelet for luck, ran her hands along the cluster of gold chains and colored beads that hung around her neck, then rolled her shoulders three times.

"Showtime," she said under her breath.

Props in hand, Massie made her way down the back stairs toward the choir pit.

When the bottoms of her burnt orange Michael Kors knee-high boots touched down on the blue carpet, Massie felt her inner diva snap into performance mode. She was ready for her grand entrance . . . almost.

First she speed-dialed Kristen.

"Why aren't you in position?" Massie hissed into her purple-Swarovski-crystal-covered Motorola cell phone.

"Where are you?" Kristen whispered back. "We thought you were bailing on us."

"Well, I'm not. I've been waiting for you at the back of the chapel for like fifteen minutes."

"Ehmagawd, I am so sorry," Kristen said. "Stand by."

Massie sighed, then snapped her phone shut. She loved how easy it was to rattle her friends.

Kristen climbed out of the choir pit and pointed the small video camera at Massie. She waved her hand, letting her subject know she was rolling.

"Shoulders back, stomach in, head up, confident smile," was the phrase Massie repeated in her head as she walked the aisle of the chapel, pretending it was the Marc Jacobs runway during Fashion Week. When she passed Kristen's camera, she turned around and signaled for it to follow her into the pit. It did.

"Hello, ladies." Massie beamed as she gracefully walked down the narrow steps to join her students. "Who's ready to learn how to make out like a maniac?"

All the girls cheered enthusiastically, except for Claire. She bit her bottom lip and tugged on her bangs. Massie shot her a warning look that said, "Stop looking so nervous or you'll give me away." Claire released her bangs and started cheering with the others.

Massie quickly swung her head around to make sure Kristen was catching the excitement with her camera. It was a great Everyone-loves-Massie shot for her video blog.

"Before we get started, I'll need everyone's payment in exact change like we discussed earlier," Massie announced. She felt a little strange taking money from Claire, Alicia, and Dylan but they knew it was going to a good cause. After collecting twenty-dollar bills from her eight students, Massie immediately stuffed the hundred-and-sixty-dollar wad into the back pocket of Kristen's rhinestone "J" Juicy Couture jeans.

"Add it to your Lake Placid fund," Massie whispered to Kristen.

"Thanks." Kristen beamed. She held her camera with new enthusiasm and pointed it at the left half of Massie's face, because *everyone* knew it was her favorite side.

The girls rearranged the dark wood stools into a semi-circle and put the only director's chair in the center for Massie. Alicia sprayed her Angel perfume to try and get rid of the stuffy dusty-old-book-and-rotting-wet-wood chapel-y smell. Only now it reeked like someone had smashed a bottle of perfume on a damp tree trunk. But it was an improvement.

"Let me start by welcoming you to MUCK, or Massie's Underground Clinic for Kissing." She plugged her mini DVD player into the wall socket and pulled a shiny disc out of a light pink plastic sleeve.

"Ehmagawd, you know what MUCK sounds like?" Olivia snickered into her delicate palm.

"Uh, yeah," Massie snapped. It should have gone without saying.

"Lovethatname," Carrie said to Livvy and Alexandra, who were seated on either side of her.

"Me too," Alexandra gushed. "It's so naughty."

Livvy's bulgy hazel eyes were fixed on Massie.

"The first thing every kissing bandit needs is a great gloss." Massie reached into her black Prada messenger bag. Seconds later she pulled out a gray Jimmy Choo shoe bag. It was filled with the stinky flavors Massie had received from her daily delivery of Glossip Girl lip gloss (her parents had signed her up for a "subscription" as one of her many Christmas presents).

She avoided the disappointed looks from Claire, Alicia, and Dylan, who knew Massie would never part with any of the good flavors. But the new girls had no idea they were getting Massie's rejects. They were beyond psyched when they were handed BBQ Chicken, California Roll, Kosher Dill, and Spaghetti Bolognese.

Livvy immediately smeared the stinky gloss on her puffy lips. "Mmmmm, it even *tastes* like sushi." She used her front teeth to scrape some into her mouth.

"How do they get pickles inside this tiny hole?" Olivia examined the tube.

"They use tickles," Layne offered. Everyone crinkled their waxed eyebrows trying to figure out whether they'd heard her correctly. "Tiny pickles."

It was such a stupid answer to an even stupider question that Massie actually laughed along with the others.

"How cute." Olivia sniffed her Glossip Girl with maternal tenderness.

"Trythisone." Carrie squeezed her tube so that a glob of BBQ Chicken oozed out. "Itsmellslikethefourthof July."

"This one is better." Alexandra puckered her shiny lips so they touched the tip of her hawk nose. She inhaled deeply. "Yummm, meat sauce. Guys are going to *hunger* to kiss me, get it?"

Dylan rolled her eyes. "So will stray dogs."

Alicia cracked up and high-fived her friend.

Massie choked down her laughter. Normally, she would have been the first to bust on Alexandra's attempt at humor but she needed these girls to love her a trillion times more than they'd ever loved Nina. Once they did, there would be plenty of time to make fun of them.

"Mine smells like an outhouse." Layne dry-heaved. "What is this stuff?"

Claire elbowed Layne in the ribs and mouthed, "Be nice."

"What?" Layne whispered to Claire. "Why?" But Claire didn't answer. Instead she turned her attention back to Massie, probably hoping Layne would do the same.

It still made Massie uncomfortable to know that someone besides her black pug, Bean, knew she was lying about her kissing experience, but if it had to be anyone, Massie was glad it was Claire. "So let's get started."

Massie turned the small screen on her portable DVD player so it faced the girls, slid in the CD, then pressed play. A slow montage of sexy photos that Massie had cut out of magazines and coffee-table books around her house and scanned into her computer flashed onto the screen, one after the other. They appeared and faded in perfect time to the dreamy beat of "Caribbean Blue" by Enya, one of Kendra's favorite New Age artists. Massie knew the girls would have no idea what they were listening to and hoped that the haunting Irish music would cast an air of romance and mystery over her presentation.

"Wow." Alexandra sighed. "This is like porno."

"Are we going to get into trouble?" Livvy asked as she chewed her lip.

"Shhhh." Carrie rolled her eyes to let Massie know she was embarrassed for her friends.

Massie took a deep breath and continued. "As you can see, everyone in these images is *kissing*." She spoke over the music. "There is kissing in advertising," she said about the Calvin Klein ad where the young couple's lips barely touched. "Kissing in art." She tapped the screen when the famous Gustav Klimt painting called *The Kiss* appeared. "And kissing in movies." And sure enough, up came a photo from the movie *The Notebook* showing Ryan Gosling and Rachel McAdams locked in a heated embrace. There were sweaty models in skimpy bathing suits passionately making out on the beach, delicate romantic kisses in ads for engagement rings, and countless perfume campaigns where the women looked into the camera instead of the eyes of the genetically perfect men they were seducing.

"Are we going to learn to kiss like *that*?" Alexandra's green, cat-shaped eyes flickered with hope. Massie noticed they were the same color as her braces and wondered if that was done on purpose.

"Which one?" Massie asked.

"All of them." Alexandra gathered her long, straight brown hair with one hand and fanned the back of her neck with the other. "I think it's important we learn all of the different styles."

"Keep it in your pants, sister," Massie said. "First you have to learn the basics."

"I agree. I always forget what third base is," Olivia said with total sincerity.

"I said the *basics*, not the *bases*," Massie said.

"Still." Olivia shrugged and slid off her tan suede blazer. She was wearing a ballet pink Petit Bateaux tank top underneath that revealed her thin, muscular arms and pointy little A-cups. They reminded Massie of Hershey's Kisses, and she suddenly realized she hadn't eaten since breakfast.

"Now, what do all of these images have in common?" Massie asked, trying to forget about her hunger.

"Is she serious?" Layne popped open a peach-flavored Go-Gurt and took a swig.

"They were all taken from your mother's magazines?" Alicia joked.

Dylan giggled. Claire bit her pinky nail.

"No." Massie sighed. "All of their lips are touching. And that's what kissing is."

Layne burst out laughing. "I want my money back."

Claire elbowed her in the ribs. "Shhhh," she hissed.

"Arc you seri—" Layne started to say to Claire but was cut off by Livvy.

"But their lips aren't touching in the painting of *The Kiss.* He's kissing her neck."

Everyone looked at Massie to see how she would handle Livvy's keen observation.

Massie could feel a familiar prickly heat under her arms. "Great call, Livvy. I was hoping someone would notice that."

Livvy sat up a little taller on her stool and playfully kicked her dangling legs back and forth. "Thanks."

"The man is kissing the woman's neck, which can be considered a kiss." Massie paused for effect. "But not a make-out."

"Ooooh." Livvy slowly nodded her head like she was finally starting to "get it."

"Massie," Carrie interrupted. "Uh, mostofusalreadyknow-thisstuff. We want to knowabouttechniques like French-kissing, lipbiting, and—"

"Kissing with braces." Alexandra turned red. She smiled shyly, showing off two rows of green wires.

"I want to know what you and Derrington have done," Alicia said.

"Yeah," Dylan agreed.

Massie looked to Claire, but Claire was too busy tugging on her uneven bangs to pick up on Massie's silent plea.

"We will get to all of that, but first it's important to learn the fundamentals," Massie said.

"Like straight-up lip pecks and open-mouthers?" Alexandra offered.

"No, like oral hygiene." Massie lifted a Louis Vuitton duffel bag off the ground and unzipped it.

"Ew," Olivia squealed. "Wait." she paused. "Isn't that third base?"

"Seriously." Livvy turned red. "We haven't even talked about Frenching yet and we're already moving on to oral?"

"OralhygieneyouidiotnotoralSEX!" Carrie snapped, and then rolled her wide brown eyes.

"Oh." Livvy and Olivia recoiled. Everyone cracked up.

"Before anyone kisses anyone, you need to know about fresh breath and healthy gums." Massie lifted up a tube of Rembrandt toothpaste and a roll of dental floss.

Alicia and Dylan busted out laughing. Even Kristen started giggling, which meant the footage would be all shaky.

"What's so funny?" Massie insisted. Claire was squirming uncomfortably in her seat and Layne had started to yawn. "You have to learn to walk before you can run."

"Correction," Alexandra said. "We have to learn to kiss before we die."

Carrie and Livvy burst out laughing.

"Hey, Alexandra?" Massie asked sweetly.

"Yeah?"

"Are you a toad?"

"No, why?"

"Then why are you acting all horny?" Massie said.

This time everyone laughed *with* Massie. "Are you getting this?" she whispered to Kristen.

Kristen nodded her head.

"Stop moving around so much," Massie hissed. "You'll ruin the shot."

"Can we skiptheteethstuff," Carrie said. "Mydadisadentist so I kindaknowaboutflossing."

"Yeah, but do you know about lip waxing and mustache bleaching?" Massie held up two different do-it-yourself facial hair remover kits. She slid off her director's chair and marched over to Carrie. Then she leaned in toward her mouth as if she were going to kiss her on the lips.

"Uh, w-what are you doing?" Carrie shifted on her stool and sat on her hands.

"Your dad may have taught you about flossing, but he failed to mention the importance of *not* having a mustache when you're a girl," Massie said.

Carrie slowly brought her hand to her face and rubbed the sides of her mouth. She turned to Alexandra. "Do I?"

Alexandra nodded slowly and with regret.

"I do?" she asked Livvy. Her voice was high-pitched and shaky.

Livvy shrugged and looked down at her knobby kneecaps.

"Now, what boy is going to want to make out with a girl that reminds him of his older brother?" Massie asked. "Females are supposed to be soft and smooth, not prickly and rugged."

Carrie started tearing up while the others pulled out their compacts and examined their faces.

Once the compacts snapped shut, Alexandra said, "The rest of us seem to be hairless, so can we get to the kissing?"

"Where was your first kiss?" Livvy asked.

"On the lips." Massie knew that wasn't what Livvy meant, but she was desperate. She had assumed these LBRs would be so happy to be in her secret club they wouldn't care what she talked about. But she had been wrong.

"Was it after the Briarwood soccer finals?" Dylan asked.

Massie wanted to slap Dylan for furthering the issue but knew her friend wasn't trying to put her on the spot. She just believed what Massie had told her.

"It was, wasn't it?" Dylan smacked her newly thin thigh. "Gawd, I am so mad I was sick that day. I knew I'd miss something good."

"Is he a good kisser, or is he all sloppy and saliva-ish?" Alicia asked playfully. "Come on, tell us something already! We want our money's worth."

Suddenly, Massie became aware of the heat from the video camera's light. It was burning her cheeks and turning her face red—she could feel it. A wave of hunger crashed inside her stomach, making her feel weak and disoriented.

"Which Glossip Girl flavor were you wearing?" Layne asked sarcastically.

The loud ringing in Massie's ears made it almost impossible for her to answer everyone's questions . . . not that she wanted to. If she didn't get out of there immediately, Massie was afraid she'd have a heart attack, or worse, start crying.

"Hold on a minute." Massie held up her finger and frantically fished through her Prada messenger bag.

The girls watched her with silent curiosity.

Massie pulled out her purple sparkly Motorola, flipped it open, and lifted it to her ear. "Yup . . . uh-huh . . . How far away is she? . . . Can you stall her while we make our escape? . . . Great." She snapped the cell phone shut and quickly dropped it in the pocket of her tweed gray-and-orange Nanette Lepore coat.

"We have to get out of here *now*." Massie ripped the plug of her DVD player out of the socket and threw her bag over her shoulder. "My lookout team says Principal Burns is on her way here to set up for a meeting she has tonight."

Layne was about to take a sip of Go-Gurt but immediately lowered the tube. "On a Friday?"

"Guess so," Massie said.

"Funny, I didn't hear your ring tone," Olivia said.

"Funny, it's called *vibrate*," Massie snapped. "I suggest we split up. A few of you should take the service exits so this looks less ahb-vious. I'll go out the main doors and if I see her, I'll just say I left my headache medicine in here after the Hillary Clinton lecture."

"That was last year," Dylan said, sounding concerned.

"Well, I'll say I have a migraine and I really need to find it," Massie said. She covered the camera lens with her hand and climbed out of the pit. Kristen, Dylan, Alicia, and Claire followed her. "Everyone else, use the other doors. Go, hurry!"

"What about the rest of the lesson?" Alexandra asked from inside the pit. "We leave for Lake Placid on Monday."

"We'll do it there," Massie shouted over her shoulder as she led her friends to safety. "I promise."

And as usual, they believed her.

Massie let out a deep sigh of relief. The fake phone call trick had served its purpose and bought her the time she'd need to retool her lesson plan. She was failing miserably as a kissing teacher, and she knew that the only way to redeem herself was to make out with Derrington before everyone figured out that she was a completely inexperienced wannabe.

It was ahb-vious to Massie that the girls had been less than pleased with their first lesson. And that certainly did not need to be advertised on a video blog. So she went back to her old system of recording State of the Unions on her PalmPilot and keeping them private.

MASSIE BLOCK'S CURRENT STATE OF THE UNION	
IN	**OUT**
Earth tones	Ring tones
Field trips with boys	Field hockey with girls
Making out	Chickening out

Claire lingered in the potpourri-scented hallway outside Massie's bedroom, trying to work up the nerve to open the door and walk in. Her hands were clammy and the insides of her stomach felt like a scene from that boat-disaster movie *The Perfect Storm*.

Earlier, when she'd walked across the grassy acre that separated the guesthouse (hers) from the main house (Massie's), Claire had asked herself why she was so nervous about attending the packing meeting and decided it was probably because she had no idea what a packing meeting was.

Claire took a deep breath and gently placed her hand on the glass knob of Massie's door, then quickly removed it, leaving a streak of sweat behind. She was six minutes late and that meant the girls could be bad-mouthing her. Not that she'd done anything wrong, but she was still paranoid. After all, bad memories take longer to heal than bloody wounds.

"One . . . two . . . three . . ." she counted inside her head. When she got to five, Claire would open the door. "Four . . ."

But a sudden burst of laughter erupted on the other side of the wall and Claire jumped back. She *knew* they were making fun of her.

Claire pressed her ear against the door.

"Did you get Krazy-Glued to the walls again?" someone behind her said.

Claire quickly lifted her head and turned around. She felt her face turning red.

"Hey, Dyl." She tried to sound casual. "What's with all the stuff?"

Dylan had bags from every boutique in Westchester hanging off her arms. Her wrists were purple from the rope handles that were digging into her flesh. But she still managed to lift the green straw in her venti Frappuccino to her lips and take a long sip.

"Ow, cold headache," Dylan squealed, and hunched over. The weight of the bags almost pulled her to the ground. Claire rushed to her side and pushed her back up.

"Thanks." Dylan's green eyes looked relaxed and playful. The red curls piled on top of her head were messy and slightly unkempt. She looked like a casual, weekend version of herself. Her jeans were loose and belt-free and the hood of her lime green sweatshirt hung down the back of her faded black Marc Jacobs blazer.

Suddenly, Claire felt some of her anxiety melt away. She liked it when the girls in the Pretty Committee looked their age—or, more precisely, *her* age.

"You saved me from getting crushed by my new wardrobe."

"Well, if you want to repay me, don't ask why I had my

ear pressed against the door," Claire said without a hint of playfulness. "And don't tell."

"Done." Dylan pointed at the door with her BCBG bag and Claire opened it without hesitation. It was always easier walking in with someone else.

Claire gasped when she stepped inside. She knew Massie never did anything unless it was headlineworthy, but this time she had outdone herself. The neat and orderly iPad had been completely transformed into an outdoor campsite. Kristen, Alicia, and Massie were sitting cross-legged on sleeping bags, staring at a stack of plastic logs that reflected flickering orange light off their faces. Marshmallows, chocolate squares, and graham crackers were being passed back and forth. The lights had been dimmed and hundreds of glow-in-the-dark stars had been stuck to Massie's ceiling. A sound effects CD supplied the greatest hits of the forest in surround sound, complete with howling wolf and babbling brook noises. An incense cone burned by Massie's bay window, filling the room with the sweet scent of pine.

Bean, Massie's small black pug, wore a pink, gray, and yellow flannel shirt and was curled up in a small stuffed canoe by the faux fire. The rest of the girls wore jeans, neutral-colored turtleneck sweaters, and red hunting caps. There was a cap laid out for Claire and one for Dylan on the two empty sleeping bags beside Kristen.

"This is awesome!" Claire knew *awesome* didn't begin to

explain how cool she thought Massie's room looked, but she was too overwhelmed to think of a better description.

"Heyyyy." Dylan yanked her clump of bags through the door frame. "Sorry I'm late—I had to buy a whole new wardrobe." She said it the way most people would say, "I had to get my warts removed."

"Why?" Massie asked. It was obvious from her devilish half-smile that she already knew the answer.

"I lost ten pounds from the flu." Dylan sounded surprised that Massie didn't already know this.

"Oh, cool," Massie responded casually.

Kristen and Alicia looked down at their glowing PalmPilots and tried not to laugh.

"It's not funny." Dylan stomped her foot. "I can't believe you can't tell." She unbuttoned her blazer and opened it like a pervy trench-coat-wearing flasher.

"We *can* tell." Alicia rolled her eyes. "It's just that you were never fat to begin with, so it's hard for us to get all psyched."

"Especially when you talk about it all the time," Massie added.

Claire sat down on her sleeping bag, picked up her hunting hat, and pretended to be very interested in the washing instructions printed on the inside—anything to stay out of the potential fight that was brewing.

"Sorry, okay?" Dylan whined. "It's just that losing weight had been my obsession for so long, and now that I did it, I have nothing to think about. I have no goals. I feel like I have lost my thing. I'm thingless."

"Come sit down" Massie waved her PalmPilot in the air. "We just started working on our packing lists. You can help us envision woodsy-chic outfits that boys will like."

"Okay." Dylan dropped her bags and raced over to the empty spot beside Kristen. "Wha'd I miss?"

Alicia tapped the screen of her Palm with the stylus pen and read her notes. "So far we've agreed on a muted color palette for tops." She tapped again. "Khakis, chocolate browns, and greens—but no limes or pastels, ahb-viously."

"I say no Juicy Couture sweats." Massie pushed up the sleeves of her chocolate brown Juicy sweatshirt. "They're so not sexy."

"But Juicy Couture jeans are okay, right?" Dylan asked.

"Dark wash only." Alicia pointed to the new dark pair of True Religions she was wearing.

Dylan crawled over her Saks Fifth Avenue bag and frantically pulled out clumps of white tissue paper. "Phew," she sighed. "I just got the new low-rise rhinestone Juicy jeans and I forgot what color the denim was."

"Well?" Alicia asked.

"I'm good." Dylan fanned her flushed face. "Thank Gawd. My new butt looks ah-dorable in them."

Claire lifted a purple pen off of Massie's desk and tore a sheet of paper from her "A Moment in the Life of Massie Block" pad.

"Do you mind?" She gestured to Massie.

Massie shook her head and slapped the air with her palm, letting Claire know she could help herself to more if she needed it.

"Thanks." Claire sat down on her sleeping bag, wishing she had a PalmPilot. She immediately put on her red cap so no one would stare at her bangs and tried to write down everything they had just said—*dark jeans, neutral tops.*

"Kristen, does this mean you're going to Lake Placid?" Dylan asked.

"No." She sighed.

Claire wanted to ask why she'd bothered showing up, but she already knew the answer. Missing one of Massie's get-togethers meant spending a sleepless night tossing and turning, wondering if you were missing anything good and wondering if anyone was saying anything about you behind your back. And nothing was worth that kind of torture.

"Hey, did anyone sign up for your memory class?" Claire tried to sound optimistic.

Kristen shook her head and looked into the faux fire.

"Maybe no one remembered," Massie tried to say with a straight face. But she lost it when everyone burst out laughing.

"Very funny." Kristen adjusted one of the many rhinestone-covered bobby pins in her hair. She was clearly trying to work with the in-between stages of her unfortunate boy cut, but the shiny stones were just drawing attention to the problem. Claire discreetly slid off her pink, glittery, stone-covered Keds and placed them behind her, just in case anyone thought the same thing about her shoes.

Claire hoped Massie would approve of them now that Mischa Barton was modeling them in all of the magazines. But why take the chance?

"Just let us pay for you," Alicia insisted.

"No, I'm fine," Kristen said through her teeth. "I think it will be fun staying here during the break. I'll get ahead on my reading, I be able to run soccer drills two times a day, and think of all the Presidents' Day sales I'll be able to hit." She stuffed a marshmallow in her mouth.

"Kristen, why didn't you send me a postcard from Morocco?" Massie asked.

"Huh?" Kristen sounded confused.

"It sounds like you were just in de-*Nile*," Massie said.

"Very funny," Kristen said. "Oh, and FYI, the Nile is in Egypt, not Morocco. I've been memorizing the globe."

"Then where's Make-out City?" Massie asked.

"Lake Placid," Dylan and Alicia shouted back.

Everyone cracked up and high-fived each other except Claire and Kristen. If Cam had responded to the poem she sent him on Thursday, Claire would have been as excited as the rest of the girls. But since he hadn't, she'd be better off spending the week with Kristen.

Suddenly the yapping sound of a small dog barking outside Massie's window drowned out the coyote calls on her sound effects CD.

Bean lifted her head, then stood up. The stuffed canoe

wobbled from her sudden movement, but she managed to jump out and run straight to Massie's bay window before it tipped.

"Did you get another puppy?" Dylan held a marshmallow to her mouth, paused, then stuffed it back in the bag.

"No," Massie said. "Maybe it's a stray."

Bean was jumping as high as she could, hoping to get a look at the competition.

"Hold on, Bean, Mommy's coming." Massie pushed herself up and hurried over to her dog. She scooped Bean up in her arms and held her in front of the window so she could size up her competition. "Kuh-laire, what is your brother *doing*?"

Claire felt her cheeks turning red. Todd never failed to embarrass her.

Bean was squirming, trying to free herself from Massie's grip. Claire sighed and joined Massie by the window. But she didn't have to look to know what was going on.

"Oh." She giggled to herself, trying to make the scene seem less mortifying than it actually was. "It's just Todd training his new robot dog, Aibo."

"In his underwear?" Massie squealed.

Alicia, Kristen, and Dylan raced over to the window. They burst out laughing when they saw Claire's skinny ten-year-old brother running around the backyard chasing a black plastic mechanical puppy. His blue terry-cloth robe had blown open, revealing knee-high gray sweat socks and a pair of loose tighty-whities.

They watched Todd dangle a round slab of bologna in front of Aibo in an effort to make him jump.

"Show 'em how it's done, Bean." Massie placed her on the floor and opened her bedroom door. They cheered when Bean raced outside. "This is gonna be good."

The girls turned back to the window and waited.

Claire tried to think of an excuse that would let her get outside to warn Todd, but it was too late. Bean was already tearing across the lawn and heading straight for Aibo. She had spent days hating that fake dog: its mechanical bark, the grinding sounds its gears made when it moved its legs, and the way its eyes would light up red when it was "awake." But now that Aibo was in danger, Claire wanted to take it all back. The dog kept Todd occupied and out of her business and that was something to celebrate, not destroy.

Within seconds, Bean swiped the bologna from Todd's fingers, devoured it, and then tore into Aibo. She grabbed him by his thin plastic tail and shook him back and forth. Todd was screaming for Bean to stop but she wouldn't.

"Massie, you should do something," Claire urged.

But Massie ignored her. She was having too much fun watching her flannel-clad puppy defend her turf. "We're in the wild now. Remember? We have to let nature take its course." It was obvious to Claire where the pug got her ferocious survival instincts.

It wasn't long before Aibo's lights went out and his body went flying across the yard.

Todd started chasing Bean around the yard.

Massie threw open her window and shouted, "Come, baby, hurry back to Mommy!"

The dog lifted her black face and raced into the house. A few seconds later, she was back in her canoe, curled up in a ball, happily chewing on Aibo's plastic tail.

"Show's over." Massie closed her window and the girls returned to their sleeping bags by the campfire.

Claire had a pit in her stomach. Part of her wanted to race to her brother's side, but she didn't dare leave the room for fear of them laughing at her while she was gone. She stuffed a few squares of chocolate in her mouth. Maybe the sugar would make her feel better.

"Okay, we have to get back to our lists. We leave tomorrow morning and I still have to pack and do a full cosmetics run," Massie said as she wheeled her mannequin into the middle of their circle. "As you can see, I dressed her for inspiration."

Claire watched the girls study the Massie-size mannequin as if they had been commissioned to paint its portrait. They tapped away at their PalmPilots as the wolves howled in the background. Even Kristen took notes, and she wasn't going, so Claire figured she should probably jot a few things down on her scrap paper.

THE OUTFIT ON THE MANNEQUIN

* Low-waisted cargo pants, army green
* Double belt thing—looks like two brown belts, but I think it's just one wrapped around twice.

* Beige, fuzzy, tight V-neck sweater. (Looks itchy.)
* Tons of tangled necklaces
* Brown fluffy moccasin boots

Deep down inside, Claire knew she wouldn't look anything like the Massie-size mannequin. Her suitcase would be filled with long johns and thick socks, and sweatshirts in forbidden pastel colors. At least this time she'd know what she was doing wrong.

For the next twenty-five minutes, Massie sat in front of her Mac typing up a list of acceptable clothing. The girls stayed close to the fire and offered up their suggestions.

"Let's start with outerwear," Massie said.

"Cropped bomber jackets with furry hoods," Dylan shouted.

"Agreed," Alicia said. "Nothing past the knees."

"Wool and cashmere coats for nights," Massie added as she typed.

"Given," Alicia said.

"Okay, footwear," Massie announced. "What are we thinking?"

"Wait," Claire said. "What about hats and gloves?" Everyone looked at her as though she'd insisted they spend the week naked. "You know, for warmth?"

"Fine." Massie looked over her shoulder at Claire while she typed. "But no ski hats or waterproof gloves. They have to be cute, feminine, and matching."

Claire sighed. "What about these red hunting caps?" She pointed to her head.

"Those are just for this meeting," Massie explained. "They're so not cute enough for the trip. I'll lend you something."

Claire's stomach leapt at the thought. She loved borrowing Massie's clothes. It was like wearing a bulletproof vest that protected her from teasing, dirty looks, and Gap jokes.

"Now, can we move on to footwear?" Massie pleaded.

Claire nodded.

"Moccasins, knee-high Uggs, and cowboy boots," Alicia insisted.

"Agreed," Dylan echoed.

"Sounds good," Claire chimed in, knowing full well she'd be wearing her tan-and-brown L. L. Bean Storm Chaser boots.

Kristen didn't say a word. She was too busy pretending to be interested in an old copy of *Teen Vogue*. She had obviously stolen it, because it said Dr. Holland on the address label.

Alicia reached behind her and held up one of Claire's sneakers. "What about rhinestone-covered Keds?"

All four girls cracked up. Claire nearly choked on a graham cracker. How long had they been holding that in? She was about to blame the tacky DIY project on Layne but decided to own it instead. The Pretty Committee girls were like wild animals: if they smelled fear, they'd pounce.

"I was wondering when one of you would notice." Claire sat up tall. "I was almost starting to think you liked them."

No one said a word.

"I'll be bringing them to Lake Placid, so if anyone wants to borrow them, let me know." Claire leaned back on her elbows and casually picked a piece of graham cracker out of her teeth.

She had done well.

"Those things are even more pathetic now that Mischa Barton is modeling them." Massie rolled her eyes. "She just misses being someone we'd like."

"Ah-greed." Dylan tried to force the red hunting cap over her thick curly hair. It stood straight up like Elmer Fudd's.

Claire burst out laughing.

"What?" Dylan squeaked.

"Nothing," Claire said. Luckily she wasn't the only one who noticed how ridiculous Dylan looked.

"You look like that hunter guy from Bugs Bunny," Alicia said.

Kristen lifted her head and giggled. "Elmer Fudd."

It wasn't long before everyone was laughing at Dylan and the focus was off Claire. She had learned a lot in the last six months.

The girls continued working on the list until Massie was satisfied.

"Done." She finally hit print and presented them all with a copy of the master packing list.

THE PRETTY COMMITTEE'S MASTER PACKING LIST
LAKE PLACID

OUTERWEAR

- Cropped bomber jackets with furry hoods
- Nothing past the knees
- Wool & cashmere coats (for nights)
- Matching hat & glove sets only (strictly for warmth)
  Nothing you would ever wear skiing

FOOTWEAR

- Moccasins
- Uggs (knee-high only)
- Cowboy boots for night
- Rhinestone-covered Keds (if you dare)

TOPS

- Sexy V-necks
- Earth tones *only*
- No Juicy Couture sweats (jeans, purses, and tops are okay)
- C&C tank tops for layering
- Cute dresses for night
- No waffle shirts or any other form of long john you might wear skiing

BOTTOMS

- Dark wash jeans
- Cords (earth tones only)
- Skirts for night (nothing below the knee)
- Tights (no black)
- No long johns

SLEEPWEAR

- Camis and boy shorts. End of story.

JEWELRY

- MASSIE ONLY: Necklaces (as many as the neck can hold)
- Diamond studs
- Gold hoops
- Rings (all kinds)
- Watches (all kinds. Even Baby G-Shock are okay, Claire ☺.)
- Brooches are so out. Leave them behind.

TECHNOLOGY

- Portable DVD players (and chargers)
- Cell phones (and chargers)
- Sidekicks (and chargers)
- Video cameras (and chargers)
- IPods/iPod shuffles/iPod minis/iPod nanos (and chargers)
- Portable speakers (and plugs)

- Bose noise-reduction headphones (extra AAA batteries)
- Digital cameras (and chargers)
- No Game Boys (antisocial. Besides, boys will have them. Good excuse to talk to them.)
- Flashlight optional (do they run on batteries? If so, bring batteries.)

UNDERWEAR
- Socks
- Bras (ALICIA!)
- Underwear (No granny panties, Claire ☺.)

COSMETICS
- Face soap
- Body soap
- Deodorant
- Moisturizer
- Powder
- Razor, shaving cream
- Perfume (one for day/one for night)
- Q-tips
- Makeup remover
- Electric toothbrush
- Dental floss
- Toothpaste
- Mouthwash
- Tweezers
- Eyelash curlers

- Mascara
- Zit cream
- Cover-up
- Visine
- Nail polish (top and base coat too)
- Nail polish remover
- Nail file
- Cuticle clipper
- Eyeliner
- Eye shadow
- Blush
- Lip gloss
- Lip balm
- Lipstick
- Shampoo
- Conditioner
- Deep conditioner
- Leave-in conditioner
- Brush
- Comb
- Hair dryer
- Diffuser
- Curling iron
- Flatiron
- Antifrizz serum
- Shine serum
- Bug spray

OTHER

- Scented candles
- Magazines
- Gum (sugar-free)
- Lavender-scented sheet spray
- Satin blindfolds for sleeping
- Slippers
- Bathrobe
- Shower cap
- Hair clips and elastics

Claire reviewed the list knowing full well the only approved item she would have was the underwear, because she'd just bought ten new pairs from Victoria's Secret.

"Remember"—Massie put her hands on her hips—"if this document is leaked, it could be very dangerous."

Claire tried as hard as she could to think of how this type of information could be "dangerous." She couldn't come up with a single thing and hoped someone else would ask, but they all seemed to understand completely.

"In case any of you aren't sure *why* this cannot fall into enemy hands, I'll explain." Massie looked right at Claire. Thankfully the room was dark, so no one could see her blush. "I went online and did a search. There are no cute stores in the Adirondacks. So if everyone starts dressing like us, we can't run to the mall and get something new. We will only have what we packed."

"Ahhh." Claire nodded, pretending to get it.

"You can always call me," Kristen offered. "I'll be shopping all week, so I can send something up in case there's an emergency."

It was obvious that Kristen was trying to sound excited about her situation, because she spoke in a high-pitched everything's-okay-with-me-why-do-you-ask? tone that Claire had never heard before.

And it was obvious by the way the corners of Massie's lips curled up that she was about to bust Kristen on her fake enthusiasm. But the *pling!* sound on her computer alerted her to an IM she had just received from SHORTZ4LIFE. And that took priority.

"Ehmagawd," Massie squealed. "It's from Derrington!"

"What'd he say?" Alicia raced over to the iMac. Massie leaned into the screen. Either she was blocking the IM from her friends or she had suddenly become farsighted. Whichever it was, she insisted that everyone stay seated. "I'll tell you everything," she promised. "I just don't need everyone breathing down my neck."

Alicia took a few steps back.

Massie read and typed.

SHORTZ4LIFE: HI BLOCK
MASSIEKUR: HEY
SHORTZ4LIFE: WHAT R U DOING?
MASSIEKUR: HANGING OUT WITH TPC

"Ask him if Josh Hotz is definitely going to Lake Placid," Alicia whispered, as if Derrington could hear her through the computer.

Claire felt her forehead break out in a cold sweat. Every time Alicia mentioned Josh, Claire tried not to look guilty. She widened her eyes and looked around the room like an innocent fawn.

MASSIEKUR: IS JOSH GOING?
SHORTZ4LIFE: ALL MY BOYZ WILL BE THERE.
JOSH, CAM, PLOVERT, & HURLEY

Claire felt her heartbeat quicken when Massie said Cam's name. More than anything, she wanted to ask Derrington if Cam had mentioned her poem, but she held back. She didn't want the Pretty Committee to know how desperate she was.

"Ehmagawd." Dylan slapped her thighs. "Ask Derrington if Plovert is still on crutches."

MASSIEKUR: IS PLOVERT STILL A GIMP?
SHORTZ4LIFE: LOL. YUP. CAST COMES OFF IN
2 WEEKS

"Love that!" Dylan said. "Now he can't run away from me."
"Should I tell Derrington you like Plovert?" Massie's fingers hovered above her keypad.

"*No!* I'm not making it official until tomorrow." She paused. "Unless you think he's a bad crush. If you do, it's no big deal. I could always go for someone else. Like Josh."

"Don't even think about it, Marvil." Alicia threw a half-chewed marshmallow at Dylan's head. "Or I'll chop off all your hair while you're sleeping and make you eat it."

Claire stuffed four squares of chocolate into her mouth at once.

"No, please don't." Dylan grabbed her own waist. "I really don't want to gain all that weight back."

"Just think," Kristen said. "If you stayed here with me, we could work out every day."

"No offense, but I'd rather eat my hair." Dylan smiled.

SHORTZ4LIFE: IS CLAIRE GOING?
MASSIEKUR: GIVEN

Claire stood up and raced over to Massie's computer. She knew she'd been asked to stay seated, but Cam was obviously asking about her. And she didn't want to miss a single word of the exchange.

"Is Cam with him?" Claire asked. "Ask him if Cam got my po—my e-mail."

Massie started typing but was interrupted by another *pling!* She started reading out loud again.

SHORTZ4LIFE: DOES SHE LIKE JOSH? CUZ HE'S TOTALLY INTO HER
MASSIEKUR: DOES <u>WHO</u> LIKE JOSH? WHO IS HE INTO?

Alicia jumped up and hurried over to the computer.

SHORTZ4LIFE: CLAIRE

Claire nudged Massie.

"Uh." Massie leaned over her screen. "He won't say."

"I need to know who it is." Alicia pleaded. "Tell him we all went home and then ask him if it's me."

"Sneaky," Kristen mumbled, and rolled her eyes.

"Ugh, will you just let me pay for your trip?" Alicia snapped. "I can't handle your attitude anymore."

"I don't want to go," Kristen said. "Honestly, I am looking forward to getting ahead on my reading."

"Fine." Alicia tried to push past Claire so she could see what Massie was typing.

Claire carefully stuck her foot under Massie's desk and knocked the plug out of the wall. The computer screen went blank.

"What happened?" Massie pushed her chair back and lifted her keyboard. She pressed every button and shook it around.

Claire pressed her elbow into Massie's back, assuring her that everything was okay.

"Gawd, that keeps happening," Massie fussed. "I have to get it fixed while I'm away."

"Can't you just call Derrington and find out who Josh likes?" Alicia begged. "Please."

"We don't talk on the phone," Massie said.

"Wait, you make out but you don't talk on the phone?" Dylan said.

"Right," Massie insisted.

A deep guttural gagging sound suddenly filled the room.

"Dylan," Alicia said.

"It's not me."

Claire looked at Massie's ceiling, silently thanking God for the distraction.

"What?" Dylan asked. "I told you, it's not me. Look." She pointed at Bean. The dog was rolling around in her canoe, choking.

Massie jumped out of her chair and raced over to her puppy. "Bean, what's wrong? What is it? Is there something in your throat?"

The dog kept gasping for air. She sounded like a car that was having engine trouble.

"Bean, please say something." Massie started tearing up. It was the first time Claire had ever seen her get emotional in front of her friends. She rubbed the pug's back in a soothing, circular motion. "Cough it up."

While the dog was choking and Massie was rubbing, Claire thought about Cam. She imagined telling him about this traumatic moment over e-mail or on the phone. He would probably get all quiet because he loved animals. And that would make Claire love him even more. *Ugh! Why won't he just let me explain? Why did I have to kiss Josh? What's going to happen when Alicia finds out?*

"Come on, sweet pea, you can do it," Massie urged. "Cough it up." Suddenly Aibo's black plastic tail shot out of Bean's mouth. "Good girl! You did it!" Massie hugged her puppy and rocked back and forth, her face buried between the dog's ears. "See, one little cough and everything's all better."

Claire covered her mouth and forced herself to cough too. But Massie was wrong. Nothing had gotten better. Her life still sucked.

"Ehmagawd," Dylan squealed as Isaac pulled into the OCD parking lot. "There's Chris Plovert." She rolled down the window of the Blocks' Range Rover and stuck her head out. "I had no idea his father drove a silver Bentley." She unzipped her cropped black bomber jacket and fluffed her red curls. "Mark the time and day," she announced. "I am officially going for Chris Plovert." She watched him struggle to get out of the backseat and giggled sympathetically. First came the tips of his silver crutches, then the cast-covered foot, and finally the rest of his Adidas-clad body.

"Close the window." Alicia tried to block the sudden breeze with her hands. "My hair is getting stuck to my lip gloss."

Dylan rolled the window down even more. "No way, it's like sixty-five degrees out. We're setting a record today. Didn't you watch *The Daily Grind* this morning?"

Alicia twisted her jet black hair into a low ponytail. "No, I was too busy tweezing to watch your mother's show."

"Just roll it up, Dyl." Massie fished through her pink Coach makeup bag. "I have to touch up my eyeliner and I don't want the boys to see."

"Massie," Isaac called over his shoulder, "please wait

79

until I've parked. I don't need you poking your eyes out while your parents are driving in the car behind me."

"If they weren't behind you, it would be okay?" Massie joked as she pressed the button that raised the glass partition between the front and back seats. She knew Isaac was just being his usual overprotective self, but she didn't have time to humor him. The Briarwood boys were a few feet away and her eyes were red and glassy. But what did she expect? She hadn't finished packing until midnight, and then she'd taken notes on William Cane's book *The Art of Kissing* so that her second MUCK session would go better than the first. If it weren't for sugar-free Red Bull, she never would have finished the whole thing. And she certainly never would have been awake at 5:30 a.m. when Jakkob had arrived to fix Claire's bangs. The early-morning house call had cost three hundred dollars but it was worth it. When he was done, Claire no longer looked like she had walked into an electrical fence. She had been transformed into one of those ah-dorably stylish French schoolgirls who have super-short bangs and cool notebooks.

Now it was Massie who needed the makeover. She looked like she had just spent a month in OCD's overchlorinated pool with her eyes open. She needed to apply Nars's Parrot Cay eyeliner to the inside of her lower lids to offset the redness ASAP.

"Do you think Cam will notice my new bangs?" Claire asked.

Massie snapped the lid over the eyeliner pencil and dropped it in her makeup bag.

"Kuh-laire." Massie sighed. "He may have one blue eye and one green one, but that doesn't mean the guy is blind."

"He's gonna fall in love with you all over again," Alicia gushed. "You seriously look cute now."

"It's true," Dylan added. "Cute in a legitimate way, not just a cute-for-*you* way."

"Thanks." Claire beamed.

"BTW, you guys have to help me find the girl Josh likes," Alicia whined.

"It's probably you." Dylan slowly shook her head, like they had been through this a million times before. "Every guy likes you."

"I know." Alicia punched herself on the thigh. "That's why this is so ahn-noying. He never talks to me."

"Maybe he's shy," Claire suggested.

"Or maybe he likes someone else," Alicia pouted.

Claire turned toward the window and bit her thumbnail.

Massie felt the familiar vibration of a text message. She flipped open her purple-crystal-covered phone and opened the car door.

She acted like she was looking at the screen, but she was really focused on the white furry moccasins she had pulled over her dark True Religion jeans. She refused to read the message until her feet were planted safely on the ground. She was still shaky from the Red Bulls, and the last thing she needed was to wipe out in front of the boys.

KRISTEN: Hve fun _ I'll miss u.

MASSSIE: Sure we can't pay?

KRISTEN: Yup thx. Enjoy the weather, nature, animals, and hiking.

MASSIE: And BOYS.

KRISTEN: That 2. xoxo

MASSIE: Enjoy the mall. xoxo

Massie dropped her phone into her metallic pink Coach tote. She knew the color violated the earth-tone-only mandate, but eventually everyone would have one and it was crucial that her public know who'd started the trend.

The Pretty Committee stood in a tight huddle on the curb while Isaac unloaded five cases of vitamin water from the hatch and Dylan's four Louis Vuitton suitcases.

Within seconds three cars caravanned into the spaces behind the Range Rover. The Blocks stepped out of a white Mercedes they had nicknamed Moby, the Riveras got out of a limo, and the Lyonses emerged from a caramel-colored Ford Taurus.

The parents unloaded their daughters' bags and suitcases from the trunks and backseats of their cars while the girls tried their hardest to look casual, like going away with boys was something they did all the time.

Members of the OCD security squad made their rounds in golf carts, picking up bags and delivering them to the luxury bus that was parked in the middle of the lot.

A cart pulled up beside them, its driver so eager to help,

he almost crashed into the red Mustang that was driven by Harris Fisher, Cam's hot older brother. The top was down and angry boy rock blasted from the speakers.

"Watch where you're going!" Harris held his fist on the horn as he pulled into the spot beside Claire's parents.

"Uh, where's your mom?" Claire asked Dylan.

"She'll be late," Dylan said casually. "Her live show ended at eight a.m. and she's coming all the way from the city. She may not get here before the bus leaves. That's why all my luggage was in the Range Rover. I thought I explained all that when I got in the car." Dylan shook her head and turned toward Massie.

"Ohhhh, right." Claire watched Cam from the corner of her eye. He was yanking a blue canvas hockey bag from the backseat of his brother's car. He turned toward his brother: they mussed each other's moppy dark hair and high-fived goodbye.

"Kuh-laire!" Massie snapped.

Claire whipped her head around. Her blue eyes were narrow with confusion, like she had just been woken out of a peaceful sleep.

"Be cool," Massie mouthed.

Claire bit her bottom lip and shrugged.

"Massie." Kendra Block tapped her daughter on the shoulder. "Is this everything?" She pointed at the five black Tumi suitcases that William had unloaded from Moby.

"Yup."

"I thought you had six bags, not five." She adjusted her

oversize Chanel sunglasses and ran her red manicured fingernails through her bob blowout.

"I do." Massie patted her pink Coach.

"Okay then." Kendra snapped her fingers at the security guard who was waiting to transport her daughter's luggage. "I guess that's it." She gave her husband, William, a stern look. He immediately pulled out his platinum Tiffany money clip.

"Take good care of these girls." William Block loosened a fifty-dollar-bill and handed it to the driver.

"Daaa-aaad," Massie groaned. She grabbed the cluster of chains around her neck and twirled them between her fingers. "This isn't an airport." She turned away from her father and rolled her eyes so her friends would know she did not approve of his ignorance.

Dylan and Alicia snickered.

"Much appreciated, sir." The security guard glanced around the parking lot, then quickly stuffed the bill into the back pocket of his navy polyester pants. He smirked at Massie as he turned the key in his cart and putt-putted toward the bus.

"LBR," Massie muttered under her breath. It didn't matter that he had no idea Massie had just called him a loser beyond repair: it made *her* feel better. "'Kay, we should start making our way toward the bus." Everyone was already there, greeting one another.

The girls quickly hugged their parents and thanked them for dropping off their bags. Then they linked arms, walked toward the bus, and didn't look back.

Massie led them straight into the center of the group and immediately began accepting her round of morning compliments.

"Massie, Iloveyournecklaces," Carrie gushed.

"Thanks, Carrie." Massie quickly looked the girl over, looking for something nice to say in return. "I love how, uh, curly your curls look today. Did you start using a new conditioner?"

"No butIrinsedwithcoldwaterinsteadofhot," Carrie confessed.

"Brilliant." Massie searched the crowd for Derrington. The bus was leaving at 9 a.m. sharp and he still hadn't arrived. *What if he changed his mind and decided not to go?* She immediately tuned into Dylan's conversation, hoping a new topic would help keep her mind off her missing crush.

"Will you *please* just breathe on me or something," Alexandra begged Dylan.

"Believe me, Alex, you don't want the flu I had," Dylan insisted.

"But you look so good now." Alexandra tapped her green braces as she examined Dylan's body.

"Thanks." Dylan batted the air like it had been nothing at all.

"Massie, you look like you've been blessed with the bug too." Alexandra turned away from Dylan. "You seem thinner than you did a few weeks ago."

Massie knew her weight loss had come from a bad case of Derrington nerves, not that she would ever admit that to

Alexandra. "Really?" Massie looked down at her legs. "I've been eating a lot of cheese lately. Maybe that's it."

"Isn't cheese supposed to be really fattening?"

"Guess not." Massie quickly repositioned herself so that she was facing Claire and Josh Hotz.

"Well, I love them." Josh tousled Claire's bangs. "They show off your big blue eyes."

Claire flashed him a fake smile, then nervously searched the crowd.

"Hey, there you are." Alicia stepped in front of Josh so she could lock eyes with Claire. "Uh, Cam's looking for you."

"He *is*?"

"Yeah, he said he wanted to talk to you about something." Alicia tilted her head to the side and widened her dark brown eyes.

"Did he say anything about an e-mail?" Claire asked.

"I know what it's about." Massie pulled Claire away.

"What is your problem?" Massie hissed. "You know she has no clue you and Cam aren't hanging out anymore. She was just trying to get you away from Josh so she could talk to him alone."

Claire shook her head slowly, silently scolding herself.

"You need to start using your brain, Kuh-laire," Massie continued, "because I am getting super-tired of looking out for you all the time. I have my own stuff to deal with."

Out of the corner of her eye, Massie noticed Chris Plovert hobbling behind the rest of the guys from the Briarwood soccer team as they hurried to greet someone.

Massie felt her stomach lurch. Derrington, the star goalie, had finally arrived.

Of course, he was wearing shorts, and not because of the record-breaking temperatures. Derrington would have exposed his knees if they were going to the Arctic Circle. It was just his thing. And as ridiculous as it was, Massie had grown to like it. Besides, his messy blond hair, light brown eyes, and beaming smile were so ah-dorable, Massie rarely felt the need to look below his neck.

Alicia sneaked up behind Massie and Claire and threw her arms around them. "Whatcha guys talking about?"

Massie got the prickly sweats under her arms. Had Alicia heard what they were talking about? "Where's Josh?"

"Ugh, the second Derrington showed he left." Alicia rolled her eyes. "I swear, Derrington's like their gawd or something."

Massie ballooned with pride. Her crush was the most popular guy in her grade. And she was the most popular girl. They were a perfect match, like DK and NY.

"But wait." Alicia paused. "What if he was just using that as an excuse to get away from me and find the girl he likes?" Her wide eyes narrowed as she scanned the crowd.

Massie crawled out from under Alicia's arm. Claire did the same.

"Why are you so sure he likes someone else?" Massie asked.

"Yeah, maybe he's just playing hard to get," Claire offered.

Massie glared at her, silently saying, "You've already done enough, let me handle this."

Claire lowered her eyes.

"You're forgiven," Massie accidentally said out loud as she casually watched Derrington high-five his soccer team buddies.

"Huh?" Alicia asked.

"Uh, nothing."

"Aloha." Olivia bounced into their circle. Her smile was wide and her teeth were so white they bordered on blue. Her super-sunny disposition and buttery blond hair were blinding. Massie slipped on her Oliver Peoples Commander sunglasses to protect her pupils from the glare.

"Sorry I'm late," Olivia said, as if anyone had actually noticed or cared. "I was working on my oral."

The girls snickered and focused on the pavement below their feet.

"My oral," Olivia insisted, "*hygiene*."

The girls snickered again.

A light breeze introduced them to a whiff of Mr. Myner's spicy cologne as he approached them. It smelled like Christmas-scented candles.

"Mr. Myner?" Massie asked in her most innocent voice. Claire, Alicia, and Olivia leaned in. "My mother insists that you are the model on our roll of paper towels. But I said you're way too busy teaching geography to model for Brawny. Am I right?"

Everyone cracked up, even Mr. Myner.

"That's sweet of your mother." His too-dark-for-February tan instantly deepened. "But you're right, Massie. I *am* too busy to model." He casually rolled back his shoulders and stretched his arms behind his back. "Not that I haven't had opportunities."

Puh-lease, Massie thought. He might have been too good looking to be a teacher, but he was way too into geography to ever be a model.

"We will be boarding the bus in five minutes," Mr. Myner instructed. "We're just trying to squeeze the last pieces of luggage inside the storage space."

"Maybe we should get another bus for luggage," Alicia suggested.

"Or maybe you girls need to be taught how to pack for a camping trip." Mr. Myner shook his head.

"We ahb-viously know how to pack." Massie pointed to the avalanche of designer suitcases that was burying one of the security guards.

"Well, then, I am determined to teach you how *not* to pack." Mr. Myner raced over to help clean up the mess. "We're leaving in five minutes." He held up a hand and wiggled his fingers.

"'Kay," they shouted back in unison.

"Olivia," Alicia said, pulling her friend's arm. "Let's do a lap to find out if anyone is talking about Josh."

"Okay."

Once they left, Claire looked at Massie. "I am so dead."

"Try to relax." Massie looked over Claire's shoulder.

Claire turned around. Layne and Derrington were coming toward them, but not together. Layne was speed walking, as if she were desperately trying to beat him to the girls. She crossed the finish line first. "Claire, I need to speak to you." She took a squirt of Go-Gurt. "ASAP."

Massie looked away in disgust. She didn't want Derrington to think she was okay with liquefied yogurt in a tube.

"What?" Claire sounded annoyed by the interruption.

"Wait, did you cut your bangs or did your forehead grow?" Layne asked.

"Jakkob had to fix them at five-thirty this morning." Claire sounded annoyed.

"They actually look cute now," Layne said. Then she remembered why she'd rushed over in the first place. Layne turned her back to Massie. "Claire, I got it," she said through her teeth.

"*What*?" Claire insisted.

Layne let her long tangled hair fall in front of her face. "*It*."

"Oh." Claire suddenly caught on.

"Please come to the bathroom with me?" Layne whimpered.

"Uh, s-sure," Claire said, her blue eyes fixed on Cam. He was leaning against the back of the bus, listening to Kemp Hurley's iPod nano and bobbing his head. "Of course."

"Uh, Claire." Massie's voice was filled with urgency. She didn't want to be left alone while Derrington was watching. It made her look like an LBR.

"Yeah?"

"Uh . . ." She waited until Derrington was standing right beside her. "Okay, then, I'll see you on the bus."

"'Kay." Claire looked confused.

"Hey, Block." Derrington's cheeks were rosy, just like his knees.

All of a sudden Massie became super-aware of everything she was doing, like she was watching herself through Derrington's eyes. She ran her fingers through her freshly washed hair, then wondered if he thought she was trying to act sexy. She fidgeted with her charm bracelet but stopped, thinking it made her look nervous. More than anything, Massie wanted to apply a fresh coat of gloss, but that was out of the question. She wanted Derrington to think her lips were naturally reflective. He could never know that her captivating shimmer came from a tube. Never.

"Look, I'm wearing your pin." Derrington lifted up the leg of his red-and-white board shorts. The rhinestone *M* pin Massie had given him two weekends ago after the soccer finals was fastened to the bottom seam, on the right side.

"Oh, no way!" Massie tried to sound surprised, but she had already seen it. It was the first thing she'd looked for when she saw him. "It looks perfect on quick-drying polyester, much better than it ever looked on my cashmere sweaters."

Derrington laughed and wiggled his butt. The gesture reminded Massie of Bean. Every time the ah-dorable puppy got excited she would shake her bottom back and forth.

"Block, you crack me up." Derrington put his semi-muscular arm around Massie's shoulder. His hand gave off an intense heat that made the muscles behind her knees go weak.

Massie shifted from one moccasin to the other. Was she supposed to put her arm around him? Or would that look slutty? Because just standing there, under the weight of his arm, made her feel like one of Plovert's aluminum crutches.

Alexandra, Livvy, and Carrie made teasing kissy-kissy sounds behind their backs, then ran away. Massie had an audience. And with that came newfound courage. The second they returned she began her performance.

Okay, Massie, you're a confident diva in three . . . two . . . one . . . aaaand action!

She lifted her arm and rested it on his shoulder. But something didn't feel right. He was taller than she was, and it felt like if he moved, her arm might get ripped from its socket.

"That's okay." Derrington reached for Massie's hand and placed it on the small of his back.

Alexandra, Livvy, and Carrie looked at one another and giggled.

Massie was so embarrassed she wanted to stomp on his foot and stab him with her *M* pin. How dare he correct her in public? Didn't he know they were being watched?

"I have to go get a seat on the bus." Massie stepped away from him.

"No one's boarding yet," Derrington pointed out.

"Exactly." Massie winked. "This is the best time." She quickly searched for a familiar face.

Dylan was just a few feet away touching up her mascara in the side mirror of a parked silver Audi. Perfect.

"Dylan, sorry to keep you waiting," Massie shouted. "I'm ready."

Dylan looked up in confusion. The mascara wand was still touching the tips of her strawberry blond lashes. "Huh?"

"I know you've been waiting for me," Massie insisted. "I'm ready now."

"Uh, cool." Dylan stuffed the green wand back into its pink tube and dropped it in her purse.

"Whatever." Derrington shook his head. "I guess I'll see you on the bus."

He walked away slowly, as if he were hoping Massie might try to stop him. But what could she possibly say? "I'm sorry I didn't know where to put my arm?" "I'm sorry I moved away from you but I don't like being corrected in front of my public?" "Wait, don't leave me?" She wanted to say it all. Instead she watched him leave.

"What's *his* problem?" Dylan asked.

Massie turned around to see if the girls were still watching her. But they were gone too. They must have assumed the show was over when Derrington left.

"Just typical boy drama." Massie sounded as if she had seen and done it all.

"You're so lucky." Dylan sighed. "I wish I had some

drama in my life. I'm so bored." She hoisted up her jeans, even though they weren't really falling down.

"It's your lucky day." Massie pointed to the black stretch limo that was pulling into the parking lot. Dylan's famous mother, Merri-Lee Marvil, was in the very back, with her face sticking out the window. Her long red curls were blowing around her pink Chanel Strass sunglasses. "Dylly!" she shouted and waved.

"Hide me." Dylan covered her eyes.

"Too late." Massie couldn't help laughing. "I think she sees you."

"Oh Gawd," Dylan moaned.

The limo pulled up beside them and the driver shut off the engine. A white *Daily Grind* van with a satellite dish on top rolled up behind them. Everyone stopped what they had been doing and focused on Dylan's famous mother.

It wasn't long before half the girls in the grade were dialing their mothers to fill them in on their celebrity sighting.

"Dyll Pickles!" Merri-Lee shouted. "You have no idea how fast we drove to get here."

Dylan's face turned the color of her hair.

"You didn't have to come," Dylan snapped in a hushed tone. But her mother was so busy smiling for her fans and posing for cell phone pictures that she didn't bother responding.

"Mom," Dylan snapped. "I hate to rush off but we have to board the bus." She hugged her mother as quickly as she could. "I'll call as soon as we get there."

"Uh, good to see you, Mrs. Marvil." Massie smiled sweetly as Dylan pulled her away. "Oh, my mother loved the piece you did on Pilates for pets."

"Well, then, I'm sure she'll adore the Mother's Day story we're about to shoot." Merri-Lee clapped her hands together with childlike enthusiasm. She looked back at her driver. He was standing beside the limo with his hands clasped behind his back. "Franco, why don't you take my bags down to that bus over there? I'm sure someone will take pity and help you unload them."

"Very well, Mrs. Marvil." He got back in the car and drove away. The white *Daily Grind* van followed.

Merri-Lee turned to face the girls. Her surgically enhanced lips curled at the sides, like she had a secret inside her mouth that was fighting to free itself.

"Bags?" Dylan asked. "Why do you have bags?"

"Surprise!" Merri-Lee threw her thin arms above her head like a Vegas showgirl jumping out of a cake. She grabbed Dylan's shoulders with her long fingers and shook her with unbridled excitement. "I'm going to Lake Placid with you."

"What?" Dylan and Massie exclaimed together.

"I know, isn't it great?" She beamed. "I'm doing a story on mother-daughter bonding, and your geography teacher said I could tag along with my crew. He's a sexy one, isn't he?"

"Ew." Dylan winced.

Massie turned her head and giggled nervously.

"Where is the mountain man? I need to introduce him to the crew." Merri-Lee snapped opened her diamond-studded compact and quickly powdered her dewy complexion. "You and I will have plenty of time to hang when we get there." She kissed her daughter on the forehead and ran away on her tippy-toes, leaving a heavy cloud of Lancôme's Trésor behind her.

"I am so not going," Dylan declared to Massie once they were alone.

"Why?" Massie snickered. "This is exactly what you wanted."

"Huh?"

"You said you needed something to worry about, didn't you?"

Dylan rolled her eyes and let Massie pull her toward the bus.

Mr. Myner cupped his hands around his mouth. "Let's go!" he shouted.

Massie could feel the prickly sweats coming back as she got closer to Derrington. Interacting with him in person was a billion times more nerve-racking than e-mailing him after school. Hopefully her deodorant was up for the challenge.

The girls from MUCK stood in a cluster, staring at the ever-shrinking space between Massie and Derrington. Once again, Massie found strength in the presence of a captive audience.

"Are we sitting together?" Massie heard herself ask

Derrington. His eyes widened and he looked around him to make sure she was actually speaking to him. "Well, arc we?"

Dylan pinched her forearm. She was ahb-viously impressed.

"Uh, yeah." He started to smile. "Totally."

"Cool," Massie said. "Let's go to the back."

The girls from MUCK made kissing noises and followed closely behind them, wanting a seat near the action.

Alicia, Olivia, Claire, and Layne had already taken all the plush seats in the back except for two, which they were saving for Massie and Dylan.

"Oh no, I guess there aren't enough seats for all of us." Massie tried to sound upset.

"That sucks." Derrington smacked one of the TV screens that hung down from the ceiling.

"Dude!" Josh shouted. "Sit here."

Derrington slid his blue backpack off his shoulder and was about to stuff it in the overhead rack when Merri-Lee butted in.

"Dylan, why don't you ride up front with me and Cole?" She giggled. "I mean Mr. Myner."

"No, thanks, I'm good," Dylan insisted. "They already saved a seat for me in the back."

"That would be perfect." Derrington grabbed his backpack. "If you sit up here, then I can sit with Block."

Massie felt his warm hand on her shoulder again. "How long is the ride?" she asked Mr. Myner.

"Five hours."

Massie froze. It would have been perfect if Derrington were a few seats away, admiring her from afar while she interacted with her friends. But sitting face-to-face with him for five hours was not something she was prepared to do. What if he wanted to hold her hand or make out?

"Come on, Pickles." Merri-Lee patted the velvety cushion next to her.

Dylan plopped herself down, folded her arms across her chest, and turned toward the window.

"Ihopeyouwaxedyourmustachethismorning." Carrie winked as Massie and Derrington passed her on their way to the back.

"What did she just say?" Derrington asked.

"Who knows?" Massie rolled her eyes.

Alexandra and Livvy smeared their lips with Glossip Girl and puckered up. It wasn't long before everyone on the bus was making kissing noises. Massie wanted to die, especially when Derrington wrapped his hands around his back and massaged his spine, so it looked like he was making out with someone. The kissing noises quickly turned to laughter.

Without thinking, Massie slapped Derrington on the butt.

"Ow." He rubbed it and gave a little wiggle.

Everyone roared with laughter. Massie blew her palm as if it were a smoking gun, stuffed it in the front pocket of her jeans, and casually took her seat, like slapping boys' butts was something she did all the time. The truth was, she'd done it to punish Derrington for making her feel so awkward and uncomfortable. But no one needed to know that. They seemed to think the slap was playful and flirty, a show of real confidence. And that was perfectly fine with her.

"What was *that* all about?" Derrington chuckled. He rubbed his butt, then slid in beside her.

"Watch yourself," Massie said, summoning her inner vixen. "There's more of that on the way if you don't behave yourself."

"Promise?" Derrington's brown eyes flickered.

Massie quickly turned to the window, pretending to have missed his comment.

"Who's ready for three days at Lake Placid?" Mr. Myner stood at the front of the bus with a proud smile.

Everyone exploded in a round of cheers and applause.

"Are you sure?" he joked. "Because there's no turning back now."

Massie sneaked a peek at Derrington from the corner of her eye. He had two freckles on his upper jaw, by his left ear. She had noticed them before and thought they were ah-dorable. But now that they were so close to her face, they seemed menacing. She shook her head and turned back to the window.

The doors hissed as the driver pulled them shut. He started the engine and eased the bus out of the lot.

Massie took a deep breath and sighed.

"You okay?" Derrington touched her arm lightly.

"Yeah, I'm fine." She gathered her hair in a ponytail, then let it fall. "Uh, I just get a little carsick. I think I need to rest my head for a minute."

"Okay." Derrington slipped off his green Burton snowboard jacket, balled it up, and handed it to Massie so she could use it as a pillow.

"Thanks." Massie tried to smile. She propped the jacket up against the window and rested her head against it. The nylon felt rough against her cheek, but Massie still managed to stay in that exact position for the next five hours.

"Smile," Claire said as she snapped another picture with her digital camera for what seemed like the nine millionth time since they'd stepped off the bus.

"It's so beautiful here," she said. It was the happiest Massie had seen her since the whole Cam incident had gone down a week earlier.

"Okay, how about one of us over here by the fire pit?" Massie reached for Dylan and Alicia. It felt weird not to have Kristen there, like Massie had forgotten to pack her toothbrush or something.

"Enough with the pictures already," Dylan snapped

She was still cranky from the five hours she'd spent listening to Mr. Myner and her mother blab on about all of the "romantic European cities" and "sensual exotic foods" Merri-Lee had been exposed to over the years thanks to her "deeply satisfying career."

"Look at the mountains behind us." Claire clicked away. "They're so big and snowy."

"Pace yourself, Kuh-laire, we haven't even seen the inside of our cabins yet," Massie said.

"I know, but this is so incredible." Claire took a deep

breath and exhaled slowly before snapping her final picture. A puff of white steam escaped from her mouth.

It was much colder in the Adirondacks than it had been in Westchester, and none of the Pretty Committee girls had dressed for the crisp mountain air. They had opted for something a little more "winter-lite" instead; tight V-neck sweaters and earth-toned turtlenecks, moccasin boots and dark jeans. Claire was the only exception, in her baby blue puffy jacket, L. L. Bean Storm Chasers, and red wool Gap turtleneck.

"Can we please go to our cabins and change?" Alicia was bouncing up and down trying to stay warm.

"Can you please keep doing that?" Chris Plovert said as he hobbled by.

Alicia folded her arms across her chest. "As soon as you learn to walk, gimp."

The girls high-fived Alicia and laughed.

The five wood cabins on Forever Wild campsite looked out on Lake Placid, a mass of fresh water that was so clean and clear you could see the red and silver rocks glistening on the bottom. The cabins formed a semi-circle around a wide fire pit that offered dozens of tree stumps as stools for sitting and roasting marshmallows. At the foot of the pit was a thin sliver of caramel-colored sand that lined the mouth of the lake like lip liner.

"Welcome to paradise," Mr. Myner said.

But no one seemed impressed. They were too busy rubbing their arms, trying to stay warm while Mr. Dingle, Briarwood's geography teacher, searched the grounds for Gus, their mysterious contact person with the keys to the cabins.

Massie was relieved that Derrington and the boys had run off to explore the hiking trails. It gave her a minute to regroup. Faking nausea for five hours had made her feel a little sick.

"Did you know Lake Placid was the site of the 1980 winter Olympics?" Mr. Myner boasted. His extra-fuzzy Patagonia pullover was still tied around his waist and he donned a pair of mirrored sunglasses with a yellow neon string attached to the arms. His nose and lips were slathered in white zinc to keep the sun off. "We are standing in the winter sports capital of the world."

"Zzzzzzzz," Massie said, barely loud enough for her friends to hear.

"You don't think this is cool?" Claire asked.

"It's cold!" Alicia stuffed her hands under her armpits.

Mr. Dingle came racing back, shaking a big round ring of keys. His big square glasses were lopsided and his potbelly jiggled as he ran. He looked like a bobblehead next to Mr. Myner.

"Who's ready to see where we're going to be living for the next three days?" Mr. Myner took the keys from Mr. Dingle and dangled them in the air like a cat toy.

"I can't believe he thinks zinc is a good look," Alicia whispered. "What an LBR."

Massie leaned in toward Dylan and whispered in her ear, "If that doesn't turn your mom off, nothing will."

"Then I guess nothing will," Dylan said. "Look." She pointed at Merri-Lee, who was in the middle of pulling the mirrored sunglasses off Mr. Myner's gooey nose so she could try them on. James, her cameraman, was right beside her, shooting.

"James," Merri-Lee hissed. "Don't get me, get the girls." She shooed him away impatiently.

"Ew." Dylan held her stomach like she was about to barf. "I'll never be able to eat again. I'll be a size zero when I get back."

Massie saw Derrington lead a pack of boys out from the woods behind the cabins. "I know what you mean."

"Ladies first," Mr. Myner said, leading the girls to their sleeping quarters. He unlocked the wooden door and they stepped inside.

"No way, this is so Ralph Lauren," said Strawberry, whose real name was Coral McAdams. Massie wasn't sure if the LBR had gotten her nickname because she dyed her hair pink or because her face was always turning red thanks to her psycho temper. She could have asked but didn't care enough to bother.

"Did you say Ralph Lauren?" Alicia said, pushing past Strawberry.

"Watch it." Strawberry elbowed Alicia.

"No, *you* watch it." Alicia held her gaze and Strawberry stepped aside and let her pass. The two girls had been temporary friends over the holidays while Alicia and Massie were fighting, and if there was one thing Strawberry should have remembered, it was Alicia's undying love for all things Ralph Lauren. She even liked his spicy Polo cologne and ah-dored Josh Hotz for wearing it.

"Ehma*gawd*!" Alicia squealed. "It is! It *is* Ralph!"

Massie was the next one to push past Strawberry. She had to see for herself.

"It is," she whispered, like she was inside an old church.

The entire room smelled like sweet pine needles.

There were five bunk beds, but not the kind you see in jail movies. These were the kind where the posts are made of hefty shellacked logs and the mattresses are thick and covered with fluffy featherbeds. Each bunk had a different, colorful Indian blanket folded across the bottom and a thick pillow at the top with a hunter green flannel pillowcase.

White fluffy sheepskin rugs covered most of the dark wood floors, except for the area around the fireplace. That was piled high with pillows and red suede beanbags. Stuffed animal heads hung above the mantel, adding the final touches to the hunting lodge theme. A row of ten cedar closets lined the back wall of the cabin, so each girl had her own personal storage area.

"Where are the bathrooms?" Layne asked.

"There are girls' and boys' bathhouses outside, right behind us," Mr. Myner said.

The girls moaned.

"Hey, we *are* roughing it, remember?" he sternly reminded them.

A loud burst of boy laughter came from outside. Massie

felt a tingle in her stomach. She couldn't believe she was going to spend multiple nights sleeping so close to Derrington and his friends.

All of a sudden, she was filled with renewed excitement. She had great clothes and a popular boyfriend, and *her* mother wasn't tagging along. It was time to stop worrying and start living.

While the girls raced to claim the beds, Massie made a silent dash for the closets. The ones on the end had more room, and she was going to need it. Besides, she knew someone in the Pretty Committee would save her a bed.

"Do you think it's Alexandra?" Alicia whispered.

Massie jumped—she could have sworn she was alone. "What?"

"Do you think Josh likes Alexandra?"

"No. Why?" Massie's heart was still thumping from the scare.

"Because she's not ugly. And she's been obsessed with learning how to kiss."

"Maybe she's just a perv," Massie said.

"Olivia thinks it's Livvy because she's good at sports and so is Josh." Alicia bit her lip. "What do you think?"

"I dunno." Massie opened a closet and ran her hands across the shelves. "Do you think this one is bigger than the one on the other side?"

"Forget it." Alicia turned away on the rubber heel of her black moccasin boot. "I'll just talk to Olivia about it."

"I'm sure she'll be a huge help," Massie called after her.

When she was alone again, Massie opened the cedar closet on the far right of the wall. It was definitely a little roomier. She immediately put her pink Coach purse inside it to mark her territory. Massie couldn't wait to unpack, get settled, and change into one of her Placid-perfect outfits.

A muscular woodsman dragged her luggage inside. The black-and-red suitcases looked great against the dark wood of the cabin. Tumi knew exactly what they were doing.

"Over here." She waved to the woodsman.

"Who do the rest of these go to?" He dropped the bags on the floor and pulled up his dirty no-name jeans by the belt loops.

"Me," Massie said impatiently. "They're all mine."

"Are you moving up here?" he asked with a toothless smile.

"Ew, no." Massie turned her back on him and rotated the dials on the lock of her sweaters-and-jeans trunk until she had had her combination all lined up, 2-3-2-6, which spelled BEAN on her phone.

A dark shadow was cast over her trunk, blocking her light. She looked up. Alexandra, Carrie, and Livvy were standing over her like three tall pine trees.

"Sowhendowegettherestofourlesson?" Carrie asked.

"What?" Massie had no clue what Carrie had just asked but could have guessed if she had to. While Livvy translated, Massie tried to accept the fact that she would have to teach another kissing clinic. So what if she had no experience, right? It wasn't like her students would know the difference, because they didn't have any either. The only thing they had ever kissed was Massie's butt.

Alexandra tapped on her green braces with her long pinky nail and jutted out her hips. "How about this afternoon?"

"How about after dinner," Massie countered. "Derrington and I need a little alone time first."

"To get warmed up?" Alexandra's face lit up.

"Ahb-viously." Massie rolled her eyes. "Now go spread the word to the rest of my students. And remember, be quiet about it."

The girls hurried off to do as they were told.

Everyone started dragging their suitcases to the closets in the back so they could start to unpack.

Claire unzipped her tattered gray wheelie. It looked like the whole bag was filled with silky bikini briefs.

"Kuh-laire," Alicia gasped. "How much underwear did you pack?"

Claire giggled. "Everything I bought at Victoria's Secret. I wasn't sure which ones I liked best so I brought them all."

"Can I have a pair?" Layne mumbled, under her breath.

"What?" Claire crinkled her pale eyebrows. "Why?"

Layne stuck out her face and squinted her already narrow green eyes. "You *know*," she insisted.

"Oh, yeah, sure. Take whatever you need."

"Yeah, while you're at it, I could use a pair myself," Alicia joked.

"No problem." Claire grabbed a fistful of underwear and handed it to Alicia. The price tags dangled off her palm. "Take as many as you want."

Massie looked up at Claire, half of her mouth curled up as if to ask what was up with the freebies. Claire widened her blue eyes and shrugged. Suddenly Massie got it. It was a guilt giveaway. Claire would continue giving things to Alicia as long as it kept her from connecting her to Josh. But Layne?

A sudden kick at the door gave way to a pack of boys wearing ski caps and Lone Ranger masks, led by Derrington.

"What's up, damsels?" Derrington leapt into the cabin and wiggled his butt for the ladies. Josh Hotz sneaked up behind him and yanked on Derrington's board shorts, revealing the top of his butt crack.

"That was for you, Massie!" Chris Plovert shouted. His cast was wrapped in saran wrap to keep the moisture out.

Derrington turned around and punched his friend in the arm. The two started cracking up and play-fighting.

Claire glanced around the room, ahb-viously to see if Cam was with them. He wasn't. She turned back to her suitcase and continued to unpack.

Massie wanted to comfort her but didn't want Derrington to think she was ignoring him.

Merri-Lee raced through the door dressed in head-to-toe fatigues that had DIOR written across the legs in what was supposed to look like yellow spray paint. "Get the boys fighting and then pan over to the girls' reactions," she demanded.

Her camera crew did exactly as they were told.

Mr. Myner politely pulled Merri-Lee aside, and after a very close conversation she smiled at him and told her crew to cut.

"Boys, get back to your cabin!" Mr. Myner shouted.

"There you are." Mr. Dingle pushed his big square bifocals up on his greasy button nose. "I gave you boys permission to take a quick trip to the bathroom, not to visit the girls."

"The next time you are caught in here you will be sent home, with a suspension," Mr. Myner said. "You are not to enter the girls' bunk, under any circumstances. And if any of you decide to take off into the woods again without supervision, you will face expulsion."

"Whoa, dude, no need to use the *E* word." Derrington lifted his mask, which made his dirty blond hair poke straight up in the air. "We were just exploring the grounds. You know, taking an interest in the topography."

He made air quotes when he said *topography*, which made Massie smile with pride. They were perfect for each other.

"I appreciate your integrity, Derrick, but there are bears back there, not to mention hundreds of miles of dense forest, and it would be very easy for you to get lost or killed or worse. And as long as I am responsible for your lives, I am forbidding you to go back there without Mr. Dingle or me.

So consider this a warning. You get no more chances. And that goes for you girls too."

"Puh-lease, like we would even want to look at the trails." Massie rolled her eyes.

Mr. Myner opened his mouth, then quickly closed it and shook his head, obviously not knowing how to respond.

"Let's go." Mr. Dingle herded the boys toward the door. Merri-Lee and her crew followed.

"See ya, Block!" Derrington shouted.

"'Bye." Massie giggled. All of the girls turned and gazed at her with the twinkle of envy in their eyes. She casually threw open the top of her suitcase, like his visit was no big deal. If only they could hear how hard her heart was pounding.

"Who do you think Josh was here to visit?" Alicia asked anyone who would answer.

Claire stuffed her face as far into her closet as it would possibly go.

"You," they all knew to say.

Alicia still seemed unsure. "You think?"

Massie spread her arms as wide as possible and hugged a pile of ultra-soft cashmere sweaters. At first touch they felt odd and slightly gooey. Like someone had sneezed on them. She lifted them up with care and caution, not quite sure what to expect.

"Ehmagawd!" she squealed. Her favorite Tocca dark green double-V-neck sweater looked like a wet poodle.

"What is it?" Mr. Myner raced over to her side.

"My Bumble and Bumble leave-in conditioner leaked all over my clothes." Massie lifted her slick hands in the air as if they were covered in blood. "Call 911. I need a dry cleaner ASAP."

Dylan and Alicia rushed to her side and started rubbing her back.

"Preferably someone who specializes in cashmere and delicates," Alicia barked at Mr. Myner.

Massie heard Layne giggle and shot her a You're-so-dead look. Layne popped open a GoGurt and took a hearty sip. Claire backed away.

Mr. Myner took a deep breath and exhaled loudly. "I'd like everyone to gather around the fireplace for a quick meeting."

"This *can't* wait." Massie could hear the panic rising in her voice. "We need to send for help immediately."

"You will need more than help if you don't do what you're told." Mr. Myner no longer sounded like "cool teacher." He had switched into "strict parent" mode right before her eyes.

Massie stood. She would have put up a bigger fight if her geography grade didn't already suck so badly, but it did and she needed Mr. Myner on her side. While he led the way to the fireplace, Massie quickly zipped up her Tumi and wheeled it with her. She refused to leave her disabled wardrobe in the back of the cabin to die alone.

"Don't worry, you can borrow anything of mine," Claire said to Massie when she sat down on a pile of colorful pillows.

Massie chuckled, like Claire had actually said something funny.

While Mr. Myner started the fire, everyone offered to share clothes with Massie, like she had recently become homeless.

She accepted their charity with grace, but deep down inside, she was still in mourning. Derrington would never get to see the ah-dorable rustic combinations she had dreamt up. Instead he would see Alicia's Sevens or Claire's turtlenecks. Unless . . . Kristen would be willing to do a quick shop-and-FedEx run for her. As soon as Myner left she would make the call and place her order.

Mr. Myner lit a match and tossed it on the tower of newspaper and logs he'd built in the middle of the pit. The tiny flame quickly became a crackling fire that shot flecks of orange embers into the air. The girls shuffled across the pillows on their butts until they were close enough to feel the heat on their outstretched hands and feet.

Mr. Myner lifted his leg onto the marble ledge of the fireplace and rested his arm on his bent knee. He looked like he was posing for the cover of *Outdoor Life* magazine.

"I have an exciting few days planned for you girls," he said. "By Wednesday you will know how to read maps, navigate using a compass, build igloos, and survive on little more than your wits and ripe berries."

Massie raised her hand.

"Yes, Massie," he said with enthusiasm. Mr. Myner loved it when his students participated and asked meaningful questions.

"Does FedEx service this area?"

"I believe so," he said, his smile fading. "Why?"

"I'm just trying to solve my clothing crisis," Massie said. "Thanks."

Mr. Myner lowered his leg and ran his fingers through his thick black hair. "Which brings me to my next point. You girls packed like you were going away for a year, not three days. And that's not going to fly with me."

Everyone looked at each other, wondering what he could possibly be getting at.

"You are here to learn how to survive in the wild, and the first lesson you are going to learn is called 'living light.'"

"That's the name of my mom's favorite spa in Boca," Alicia announced.

The girls instantly perked up, thinking they were about to spend the day getting spa treatments.

"Well, my version is about doing away with excess," Mr. Myner said. "You'll be surprised by how little you need to live a happy, meaningful life."

"Principal Burns needs to give the poor guy a raise," Dylan whispered to Massie.

Massie bit her lower lip to keep from laughing.

"So I want each one of you to pick out two pairs of pants, two sweaters, two long-sleeve jerseys, three pairs of underwear, and one pair of boots. The rest of your stuff will be taken away and locked in the bus until it's time to leave. And oh . . ." Mr. Myner let out a small smile. "Try to avoid white or anything with stripes, because I'm told they don't look good on camera."

Dylan hid her face in her hands and shook her head.

"Sounds cool!" Strawberry blurted out. Her excited expression changed the instant she realized she was the only one in the room who felt that way.

"No, it doesn't!" Alicia shouted. "Not only are we going to be on TV wearing the same outfits every day, but there are *guys* here. Why should they see us in the same clothes day after day? It's not fair to *them*."

"I assure you, they will be following the same rules," Mr. Myner said.

"This is a Board of Health issue," Dylan protested. "It's not sanitary."

"You will be taught to wash your clothes in the lake with Ivory soap. It's biodegradable, you know." Mr. Myner held up his index finger. "And I assure you, there is no fresher water source in the entire state."

"Most of my stuff needs to be washed in warm water, and that lake is freezing." Livvy shivered as she bit down on her bottom lip.

"How are we supposed to explain this to the clothes we leave behind?" Olivia asked. "They're going to be so upset."

Everyone giggled.

"What about all the money we spent buying new wardrobes for the trip?" Alexandra asked. "Will we be compensated for that?"

"Your parents got a newsletter that explained all of this." Mr. Myner stroked his mustache.

"Puh-lease, no one reads those." Massie rolled her eyes.

The girls nodded in agreement.

"Whatifsomethinggetsstainedorsoiledormuddythenwhat?" Carrie shouted.

"What?" Mr. Myner sounded frustrated. "Ladies, this is a survival trip, not Fashion Week. You'll see it's very liberating. Trust me, at the end of our time here, you'll thank me."

"How does he know about Fashion Week?" Alicia whispered to Massie.

"My mom," Dylan suggested.

Layne tore the top off another Go-Gurt. It must have been her fifth one of the day.

"Which reminds me," Mr. Myner said. "I will be collecting your food stashes. Not only does stuff like that attract bears and rodents, but also an endless supply will keep you from feeding off of your existing fat stores in case of a crisis."

"The only fat store I know about is Lane Bryant," Massie said.

The whole class burst out laughing. Even Mr. Myner smiled.

"Seriously, though," Dylan shouted above the laughter. "What if you don't have any fat stores?"

Massie and Alicia rolled their eyes.

"Trust me, you do," Mr. Myner said.

Dylan folded her arms across her chest and stuck her tongue out at him the second he looked away.

"Do I need to remind you that your performance on this trip is worth extra credit?"

The girls immediately turned to one another to discuss what to save and what to surrender. While they debated, Mr. Myner made the rounds with a big green garbage bag. One by one they reached into their handbags and dumped their bubble gum, sugar-free gum, Luna bars, yogurt bars, wheat-free bars, carob chocolate bars, and baked Lays into the bag. Layne tossed her tube of Go-Gurt in and swore up and down that it was her last.

"If it's all right with you, Ms. Block, we took the liberty of leaving your five cases of vitamin water on the bus."

"Whatevs." Massie shrugged.

"Next I am coming around for all of your electronics, so please have those out," he said. "Cell phones, Sidekicks, BlackBerries, video games, DVD players, and computers— all of it. A violation buys you a ticket home, no exceptions."

Mr. Myner ignored the enraged protests that followed and stayed his course.

"And another thing," he said. "Claire and Layne, you will have to get rid of your glittery shoes." He pointed to their rhinestone-covered sneakers. "They attract bears and other wild beasts."

"Yes!" Massie lifted her hands above her head and punched the air with her fists.

Layne sighed and started picking the black rhinestones off her Chucks. Claire simply took hers off and dumped them in his trash bag.

"You too, Massie," Mr. Myner said.

"Ew, puh-lease, I would never wear glittery sneakers," Massie insisted.

"Your necklaces," he said. "The light reflects off them as well."

"I can't." Massie grabbed her chains like they were her life support.

"You will." Mr. Myner held out his hand.

Massie ran her fingers through the gold tangles around her neck, separating one chain from the other. When she found the one she was looking for, she held it in the air like an Olympic medalist showing off her gold. "This one has a compass. And I'll need that out here."

Mr. Myner stepped over the girls on the floor on his way over to Massie. She held the round gold compass in front of his face while he examined it closely. He lifted it in his manly chapped palm and turned it in every direction to make sure the needle moved.

"Ow, you're choking me." Massie rubbed her neck.

"Fine." Mr. Myner dropped the compass. "But the rest have to go."

Massie grinned. In the context of this day, she considered this a major victory.

"You have exactly ten minutes to wash up and dress warmly. I'd like to see you all in front of Powwow Log at fourteen hundred hours. That's the big stump to the right of the dining pavilion."

Olivia raised her hand.

"Yes, Olivia?"

"My watch only goes up to twelve," she said.

Everyone laughed. Olivia looked around with a confused expression on her face.

"Fourteen hundred is military time for two o'clock," Mr. Myner said kindly. "I will be happy to explain how it works if you'd like."

"Nah." Olivia waved him away. "It's not like I'm going to join or anything, but thanks anyway."

Mr. Myner raised his voice so he could be heard over the laughter. "The Adirondack park patrol will stop by to remove your excess luggage and put it in storage. Please cooperate with them." He turned the knob on the cabin door and looked back at the girls with a satisfied smile on his face. "Welcome to paradise!" He threw open the door and breathed in the crisp, sun-drenched mountain air. "Ahhhhh." He exhaled, then left.

Massie reached for her PalmPilot to enter her latest State of the Union only to realize Mr. Myner had confiscated it. Maybe Kristen didn't have it so bad after all.

"I bet she's memorizing *TV Guide*." Alicia buttoned her gray cashmere Ralph Lauren coat.

"I bet she's checking out the sales at Target," Dylan guessed.

"You're all wrong," Massie said. "She's probably working on her college admissions essay."

While the girls played guess-what-Kristen's-doing on their walk to Powwow Log, Claire tried to focus on the rhythmic sound of twigs snapping beneath her two-toned boots. It was a little game she'd just invented called step 'n' snap. The object was to crack a twig with every step she took. It was her latest attempt to take her mind off of Cam and focus on something else. But it wasn't working. Didn't he miss her at all? Was she that easy to get over?

Cam's unmistakable snicker instantly distracted her—a cross between a giggle and a rusty jackhammer. He was standing ten feet away on Powwow Log, with his hands stuffed into the side pockets of his brown leather jacket. He was kicking his heels into the thick, dry wood and talking to Plovert, who was leaning on a crutch, trying to stay balanced on the soft ground.

"Look how tough he is." Dylan tapped her heart when

she saw Plovert. "One working leg and he's out here braving the elements."

"Why don't you go over there and tell him how you've been madly in love with him since eight-thirty this morning?" Massie gave Dylan a playful shove.

"Shut up!" Dylan smacked Massie lightly on the arm.

Within seconds the two girls were throwing pine needles in each other's hair and laughing hysterically.

Claire wondered if they knew they had an audience, then assumed they did. Massie rarely did anything without one.

"Catfight!" Derrington shouted as he approached the log with Kemp Hurley and Josh Hotz. Five other guys lagged behind them, but Claire didn't even know their names. According to the Pretty Committee, they didn't count because:

1) They never bothered to flirt.
2) They weren't on the soccer team.
3) They were barely tall enough to turn on a light switch.

"Watch out," Massie shouted. "We're coming for you next."

Claire admired Massie for being able to act comfortable around Derrington even though she wasn't. How did she do it? If only Claire could pretend to be happy without Cam. But it was impossible. Every time she tried, her voice sounded higher than usual and her movements felt foreign and exaggerated, like she was watching a bad actress play the role of Claire Lyons in the movie version of her pathetic love life.

"Bring it!" Derrington put up his dukes and punched the air.

"Hold me back." Massie pretended to lunge toward Derrington but stayed close to her girls.

"Relax." Mr. Dingle jogged up behind Derrington, grabbed his fists, and lowered them. "We're not here to beat up the girls."

"We're not?" Derrington wiggled his butt.

The boys laughed. A light breeze blew Cam's thick dark hair to the right of his face, revealing his blue eye. Claire sighed. She knew it would be a matter of days before another girl stole him away for good.

"Let's hang here," Massie declared. The girls stood under a tree a few feet away from the log. Now that Massie had marked her turf, it would be the Pretty Committee's spot for the rest of the trip. When Alexandra, Carrie, Livvy, Olivia, and Layne showed up a few seconds later, they automatically knew to keep a reasonable distance. The only one stupid enough to stand right under the tree was Strawberry. She walked right over to the girls and started chatting like they were all the best of friends.

"So, what do you think our first activity is going to be?" she asked.

"I heard we're all going to stand around and watch Mr. Myner pitch a tent." Massie tried not to laugh at her own joke, but she lost it the second Dylan and Alicia cracked up.

Claire felt bad. It was obvious Strawberry didn't get it because she just stood there, then nervously grabbed a handful of her pink hair and stuffed it under the hood of her gray sweatshirt.

"It's so funny how the boys are standing by the log and we're back here by the tree," Claire mused.

Massie, Dylan, and Alicia looked at her, their eyebrows raised.

"Why?" Massie sounded slightly annoyed. "How *should* it be?"

"Well, at my old school in Orlando everyone would be together."

"Perv," Alicia sneezed.

Dylan cracked up.

"Oh, that'll happen," Massie assured her. "You'll see."

Claire regretted having said anything, knowing Massie would now make it a point to force the sexes together just to prove that OCD was as cool as any public school in Florida.

Mr. Myner and Merri-Lee walked out of the dining pavilion laughing, the two-man camera crew following closely behind.

Mr. Myner's smile faded when he noticed that everyone was on time. "Sorry we're late. I had an important meeting with the chef."

Merri-Lee rubbed her flat belly, licked her lips for the camera, and gave it a thumbs-up.

"If they were eating while we were left out here to starve, I'm suing." Dylan folded her arms across her chest.

"I doubt they were eating," Strawberry chimed in. "It looks like your mother hasn't had a meal in five years."

"Say one more thing about my mother and you'll be speaking out of your butt."

Strawberry lifted her hand in the air and shook it, to joke about how nervous she was. Then she went to join the other girls on the outskirts of the tree.

Merri-Lee waved at her daughter and mouthed, "Hi, Pickles."

"Gawd, I'll never make out with Plovert as long as *she's* here," Dylan moaned.

Cam jumped off Powwow Log when Mr. Myner and Mr. Dingle stepped up.

"Okay." Mr. Dingle clapped his hands, then quickly rubbed them together. "Who's ready to get started?"

"What about lunch?" Kemp Hurley shouted. His hands were in the pockets of his baggy skater pants and he swayed from side to side.

A chorus of *yeah*s rose up from the crowd.

"Lunch comes after," Mr. Myner explained.

Everyone groaned.

"It's all part of surviving. I need you hungry and motivated."

Merri-Lee stood beside Dylan, put a bony arm around her, and smiled for the camera, like this was how they always stood. Dylan shook free immediately and rolled her eyes.

Mr. Myner rested his man-hands on his hips and waited for silence before he continued.

"We are going to divide you into three different survival pods and those are the people you will be working with this afternoon. They are your lifeblood. You must work together to traverse the terrain, interpret the maps, and reach the final destination."

Mr. Dingle jumped in. "The first pod to arrive will get a gourmet lunch in the dining pavilion, consisting of lobster mac and cheese, Caesar salad, and prime rib with herb-and-butter sauce. For dessert you will have your choice of bananas Foster, deep-fried ice cream, and double-fudge chocolate brownies. The losing pods will be served deviled eggs and saffron rice by the outdoor fire pit. No dessert. Aaaand the winners will also go on a hot air balloon ride so that they can admire the park's breathtaking topography."

Everyone started talking at once until Mr. Myner put his hands on his hips again.

"Now, these maps are very basic. We've been teaching you how to read them in class for the last two weeks. If you've been paying attention, your only challenge will be working together." Mr. Myner pulled a rolled-up stack of papers out of his back pocket and handed them to Mr. Dingle, who just stood there, looking from the maps to Mr. Myner, then back to the maps.

Mr. Myner thrust them in front of Mr. Dingle's face. "The fabulous Mr. Dingle will hand out the maps while I divide you into your pods."

Mr. Dingle must have loved being called fabulous,

because he finally wiped the offended look off his face and lifted the maps above his head.

Claire took her copy and examined it closely. It looked pretty simple. Some squiggly lines that indicated a river, a few solid black lines that represented the different trails, and a circle in the bottom left-hand corner of the page that must have been their endpoint. How hard could this be? Claire's mouth watered as she pictured herself digging into a steaming bowl of lobster mac & cheese.

"Pod one," Mr. Myner announced, "is Alexandra Regan, Kemp Hurley, Livvy Collins, Derrick Harrington, Steven Parker, and Dylan Marvil. Your captain is Paul Danno."

"Who's *that*?" Dylan hissed.

Massie, Alicia, and Claire shrugged.

"Uch, there's *no one* on my team," Dylan sneered.

"You have Derrington," Massie whispered.

"And how does that help me*?*" Dylan snapped. "Last time I checked he was *your* crush."

Massie shrugged.

"Don't worry, Pickles." Merri-Lee pinched her daughter's butt. "I'll be with you."

Dylan rolled her eyes and left to join her LBR group. Merri-Lee and her crew hustled to catch up.

"Pod two," Mr. Myner continued.

Massie, Alicia, and Claire held hands, hoping they'd be together.

"Claire Lyons, Olivia Ryan, Josh Hotz, and Cam Fisher, and your captain is Coral McAdams."

Strawberry jumped for joy. "I love that I'm captain!" She stuck two fingers in her mouth and whistled. "Over here, team!"

Claire looked at Massie and silently begged for help. Cam *and* Josh? She didn't know if she should celebrate or tie a rock to her leg and walk straight into Lake Placid.

"Olivia," Alicia whispered.

"Yeah." Olivia stepped under the tree.

"Find out who Josh likes," Alicia ordered. "But don't let him know I want to know."

"Given." Olivia nodded. "Come on, Claire."

Claire looked back at Massie one last time, but all Massie could do was wave goodbye with a half-smile on her face. Was she actually enjoying this?

"Pod three is Alicia Rivera—"

"You're hot!" shouted one of the boys.

Mr. Myner ignored the interruption. "Carrie Randolph, Layne Abeley, Marc Cooper, B. J. O'Brian, Adam Freeman. Your captain is Massie Block."

"Wait, what about me?" Chris Plovert asked, perplexed.

"I thought you might want to sit this one out because of the leg," Mr. Dingle said.

"No way, man," Plovert snapped. "That's discrimination. I can do this."

"Are you sure, Mr. Plovert?" Mr. Dingle pushed his glasses up his nose. "It *is* a race, you know."

"I know."

"O-kay." Mr. Myner sounded doubtful but willing to give

Plovert a chance. "Who would like to welcome Chris to their team?"

No one volunteered. Not even Dylan.

"Aw, come on, guys," Chris pleaded.

"Dude, we're playing for fooood." Kemp rubbed his skinny belly. "No hard feelings, but you gotta understand."

"He can come on our team," a sweet voice offered.

Chris's face lit up when he saw that it belonged to the beautiful Olivia Ryan, the blond half of the Twenty.

Dylan stomped her foot and scowled.

"O-livia," Strawberry snapped. "What are you doing? I'm the captain and I say who joins this team."

But it was too late. Plovert was already hobbling over.

"You just kissed our chance at a good lunch goodbye." Strawberry punched the trunk of a spruce tree. "What were you thinking?" Her face turned dark red.

"Trust me, it's part of my strategy," Olivia whispered. "If one of us gets hurt, we'll have a pair of crutches." She winked. "How smart is *that*?"

Strawberry punched the tree again while the rest of her pod welcomed their newest member.

"Are all pods ready?" Mr. Myner asked.

"Ready," everyone said, almost at the same time.

"On the count of three I want you to head toward the back of the cabins and find your pod's trailhead. I have marked a different entry point for each: green for pod one, blue for two, and yellow for three. Ready? One—"

And they were off.

Strawberry marched ahead of her pod, tearing down every leaf and branch that crossed her path. She swung her arms like the speed-walking mothers that Claire and Massie always passed on their way to school.

"Let's go, people!" Strawberry shouted without turning around.

Claire looked at Cam and rolled her eyes, hoping he would join her in making fun of Strawberry, but he immediately looked up at the blue sky. It was obviously going to take more than an eye roll to win him back.

The thick woods swallowed up the competition's voices and crunching footsteps as they all went their separate ways. Soon silence hugged them like a sleeping bag. Claire wondered if anyone could hear how hard her heart was pounding.

"Hey, Claire, want me to take your picture?" Josh scurried up beside her and pulled a digital camera out of his blue wool pea coat. He twirled it around his finger by its gray string.

"Hey, how'd you get that?" Claire stopped and looked into his warm dark brown eyes. "Mr. Myner *took* mine."

"I didn't tell Dingle I had it." His eyelashes were so thick and dark, Claire wondered if he was wearing mascara. And then she realized why Alicia thought he was so cute: he looked exactly like her.

"I wish I'd thought of that." Claire kicked a pinecone. It accidentally hit the back of Strawberry's hiking boot.

"Let's go, people!" she shouted again. "Less kicking and more walking, please."

Claire snickered and looked at Cam again, but Josh was blocking him.

"I feel so bad you don't have your camera." He shook his head and smiled affectionately. "You're too honest. That's what I like about you."

Claire whipped her head around to see if Olivia had heard that. If *she* had, then Alicia would, and . . . The rest was too terrifying to think about.

But Olivia was too busy scraping a mud clump off the end of Plovert's crutch to hear.

"Hey, Strawberry, can I take a look at that map?" Cam shouted as he ran ahead. A faint trace of his sweet-smelling Drakkar Noir cologne lingered behind in his absence. Claire inhaled deeply as she moved through it, hoping to reclaim a little piece of him. But Josh inched closer to Claire. Now that Cam was gone, Josh's spicy Polo cologne seemed to chase the last bits of Drakkar away for good.

"Who's hungry?" Strawberry barked.

"Me," everyone answered at once.

"THEN MOVE!"

Two white-breasted sparrows darted out of their nest and everyone jumped.

"Relax," Plovert said. "You're scaring the wildlife."

"Less talking and more hopping, gimp-boy," Strawberry hollered.

Olivia and Plovert scurried to catch up.

"So, Josh." Olivia cut Claire off the narrow trail so she could walk beside him. "Let's play a game."

"Can I play?" Plovert was out of breath.

"Later." Olivia quickly dismissed him. "You need your energy right now to keep up. This game is just for Josh."

"Uh, okay." Josh sounded a little afraid.

Claire could barely see Cam. He was up ahead with Strawberry. Did he like *her*? Maybe he thought her pink-dyed hair was edgy and cool. What if she liked the Strokes as much as he did? What if they were talking about their favorite Strokes song right now? She searched her mind for an excuse to catch up to them.

"Okay, Josh, I'm going to name two girls and you tell me which one you would rather lip kiss," Olivia said.

"'Kay." He tucked his camera away and stuffed his hands inside his coat pockets.

"Jessica Simpson or Ashlee?"

"Jessica."

"That one was easy," Plovert shouted.

"Okay, how about Principal Burns or Hillary Clinton?"

"Ew, neither." Josh made a face like he had just sniffed dog poo.

"You have to pick one, that's the game."

"Fine, Hillary."

"Good. Okay, Strawberry or, uhhhhm, Alicia," Olivia whispered.

Claire suddenly realized what Olivia was doing. It was a clever yet subtle way to figure out who Josh liked.

"Alicia," Josh answered.

"What about Alexandra or Alicia?"

"Is Alexandra the one with the green braces?" Josh asked.

"Yup."

"Alicia."

Olivia smiled to herself.

"Carrie, Livvy, or Alicia?"

"Alicia."

"Layne Abeley or Alicia?"

"Alicia."

"Nice." Olivia smiled.

"Claire or Alicia?"

Claire and Cam stopped walking at the same time. This was not happening. Please, no!

"Don't you want to give Plovert a chance to play?" Claire quickly chimed in.

"Yeah, ask me one," Plovert huffed.

"Okay, Merri-Lee Marvil or me?" Olivia's short attention span had never been more appealing.

"Dylan's mom or *you*?" Plovert asked.

"Come *awn*, you guys," Strawberry whined. "Focus."

Cam and Claire started walking again.

"Yeah." Olivia giggled. "Merri-Lee or me."

"You."

"You liiiike me. You liiiike meeee," Olivia sang.

"Hey, that's not fair." Plovert pretended he was angry. Then he fell. "Owww!"

Everyone stopped to help him up. But as soon as he was standing, he fell again. Strawberry checked her manly Seiko diving watch and sighed while Cam and Josh lifted him back up.

"You okay, man?" Cam's hand was still resting on Plovert's shoulder.

"Yeah, thanks." Plovert looked at Olivia and turned red. "I'm fine. I think the doctor gave me a pair of bum crutches."

"You should sue him," Olivia suggested. "Alicia's dad is a very successful lawyer. He can help."

"Plovert, buddy." Cam studied him. "Try to take it easy."

Claire found herself wanting to trade places with Plovert. She would have gladly taken a broken leg if meant Cam would be nice to her.

"Hey, Josh." Olivia beckoned. "Did you know Alicia's dad was a successful lawyer?"

"Uh, no."

"Well, he is." She nodded slowly, like she was giving him some very privileged information. "*Very* successful."

"Cool." Josh smiled politely at Olivia. He obviously had no idea how this information related to him.

Strawberry and Cam stopped walking once they came to a fork in the road. One trail led up into the woods and the other continued along the lazy river. They pored over the map, trying to decide which way to go.

"Hurry," Olivia urged. "I'm getting hungry."

"We're trying," Strawberry barked.

Claire expected her to scold Olivia for complaining and not helping. But Olivia's flowing blond hair, navy eyes, and clear white skin made her look like a fragile woodland fairy. And Strawberry probably thought it was wrong to shout at someone who looked so innocent.

"Why don't we just follow the sound of those cheering voices and go left," Plovert suggested. He was leaning on his crutches, with his head cocked to the side.

"What cheer—" Cam started to ask but stopped once he heard them.

"Who's that singing about loving mac and cheese?" Olivia asked.

"Dylan," Claire confirmed.

"Sounds like we lost." Strawberry sulked. She turned left and everyone followed in silence. "It's not like we didn't try, right? I mean, Olivia, you were great at finding out who Josh wants to kiss. And Plovert, every time we started to pick up speed you really helped out by falling. And Claire—"

"All right, enough," Cam snapped. "We lost a stupid race—it's no big deal."

Had Cam just defended her? Claire felt a jolt shoot through her body. It recharged her. It made her want to sprint through the woods as quickly as she could. It made her want to hug Cam and sniff the side of his neck.

Strawberry karate-kicked a low tree branch. It snapped and dropped to the ground. "Loser!" she shouted at the fallen wood, then stormed off.

Claire picked up her pace, quietly leaping over errant logs and rocks so she could catch up to Cam without sounding like she was trying to. In a matter of seconds she was back in the Drakkar zone.

"Thanks for coming to my rescue." Claire felt her hands go clammy. It was the first time she'd spoken to Cam in days.

"It was no big deal," Cam said to his beat-up hiking boots. "I was just tired of hearing her voice."

Then he sped up.

Claire stopped walking and hunched over. She couldn't tell if Cam had really punched her in the stomach or if it just felt like he had.

"You okay?"

She felt Josh's hand on the small of her back.

"Fine, thanks." Claire straightened up and hurried down the trail.

She was one of the last people to step into the clearing. Almost everyone else beat her to it and was either celebrating their victory or mourning their loss.

"Congratulations to pod number one. You really worked well as a team," Mr. Myner announced.

"And my crew got some great shots of you boys crossing

the river," Merri-Lee added. "It was like *The Amazing Race*," she gushed.

"Fixed," someone coughed.

"Fixed," someone else coughed.

Suddenly everyone was coughing, "Fixed," because Dylan's team, the only one with its own camera crew, had happened to win.

"Jealous," Dylan coughed back. Her teammates joined in.

"All right, that's enough." Mr. Myner raised his hand. "Nothing was fixed. Team one showed some wonderful ingenuity. You could all learn something from them. While they are enjoying a delectable gourmet lunch, the rest of you will eat by the fire pit. After a short break, Mr. Dingle will take you back into the woods for a quick tutorial on map reading and I will lead the hot air balloon expedition. Have a good afternoon, everyone."

The losers, including Mr. Dingle, groaned while the winners jumped up and down and hugged one another.

"Hey, Block," Derrington shouted from the winner's circle. "Aren't you going to give me a kiss goodbye?"

Everyone stopped and faced Massie. But she just stood there with a shocked expression on her face. Claire looked away. It was hard to see Massie at a loss for words. It seemed unnatural.

"What if I die in the air balloon?" Derrington said. "It may be your last chance."

Massie took off her Oliver Peoples sunglasses and tapped one of the arms against her bottom teeth. Claire could tell she was trying to think of a comeback, but everyone else probably thought she looked like a seductive movie star.

"Derrick." Massie pronounced his name like a disappointed teacher. "Are you having a soccer finals flashback?"

"What?" Derrington was confused. "No, why?"

"Because you seem a little desperate to score," Massie said.

The Briarwood soccer boys busted out laughing and messed Derrington's hair.

"She totally dogged you!" Kemp smacked his own thigh.

"Your loss, Block." Derrington looked genuinely hurt.

Massie must have picked up on this too, because she quickly moved closer to him and softened her tone.

"Look," she whispered. "I just think it's a little tacky to kiss in public, especially in broad daylight."

"So then later?" Derrington raised his eyebrows.

"Later." Massie turned and walked back to her friends, but the MUCK girls got to her first. They couldn't wait to congratulate her on her performance.

"This way." Mr. Dingle waved the losers toward the trail back to camp.

"What's wrong with you?" Layne asked Claire as the defeated group walked back in silence.

"Nothing." She didn't want to talk about Cam because if she did, she'd start bawling. Besides, he was only a few steps ahead of her, helping Plovert. "How was your morning?"

"Awful," Layne whined. "I have the worst cramps from you know what. It feels like I swallowed a squirrel and now it's trying to claw its way out through my belly button."

"I can totally relate." Claire sighed.

"Huh?" Layne knitted her eyebrows.

"Hey, Kuh-laire," Massie called.

"Yeah?" Claire quickly played back the last twenty-four hours in her head, trying to figure out if she was in trouble.

"Fall back," Massie insisted.

Claire stopped and let everyone pass. Once there was a safe amount of space between them and everyone else, Massie spoke. "I need your help."

"What?" Claire wasn't sure she'd heard right. Massie never needed help.

"Shhhh," Massie insisted. "What I'm about to ask you goes to the grave, 'kay?" She held out her pinky. Claire lifted hers and they shook.

"What is it?"

"I need you to teach me how to kiss," Massie whispered.

"*What*?" Since when did making out with Josh Hotz once make her an expert?

"Pleeeease."

Claire searched Massie's amber eyes. *Was she joking?* But there was no flicker of mischief and no innocent eyelash batting. This was real.

"Massie, I—"

"Please," Massie begged.

Claire wished someone had been around to witness this moment. She had always fantasized about Massie desperately needed her for *something*, but never *this*. For the first time in their relationship Claire was in a position of power over Massie. And she intended to take full advantage of it.

"Okay." Claire straightened her shoulders and raised her chin in the air.

Massie sighed.

"But only if you do something for me."

"Anything," Massie promised.

"I need you to help me get Cam back," Claire said. "Before he ends up liking someone else."

"No problem." Massie sounded like she already knew exactly how she was going to pull it off. "Done."

"Done," Claire answered back, feeling like she had just made a deal with the devil.

One she had no idea how to repay.

Massie turned on the four battery-powered heaters she had swiped from her cabin and placed them around the igloo. She wanted Claire to feel warm when she arrived for their private kissing lesson.

Earlier that afternoon Mr. Myner had taught them how to build igloos by cutting blocks of snow and packing them to form circular walls. But no one's was as spacious and comfy as Mr. Myner's, so Massie had opted to hold her underground meeting in there. She sneaked out of dinner early to decorate it with sheepskin rugs and beanbags from her cabin. And for ambience, she placed eight red cinnamon-scented candles evenly along the floor near the walls. It wasn't like anything in the ice palace could catch on fire. Igloo decorating had its advantages.

By the time she blew out the last match, the heat was blasting. What had once been a frigid ice hut was now a warm and inviting secret clubhouse. All Massie could do now was wait for Claire and try to stop imagining a hungry family of black bears circling outside, licking their lips.

Finally, dinner let out. The wood doors of the dining pavilion squeaked open, giving way to a swell of simultaneous conversations and laughter. It was break time. And everyone would be going back to their cabins to digest and change into their pajamas before the nighttime bonfire reading of *Hatchet*—a novel about a thirteen-year-old boy who survived a plane crash and had to learn to fend for himself in the Canadian wilderness. Massie peered out of the semicircular doorway knowing *her* survival depended on Claire and her kissing lesson.

Suddenly Massie heard a deep voice. "Uh, hello ma'am, mind if I join you?"

Massie looked up and shrieked. There was a giant moose head in the doorway of the igloo and it was staring straight at her.

"Relax." Claire giggled. "It's me." She hunched over and squeezed through the narrow opening, then turned the moose sideways so his antlers wouldn't chip the walls. "Wow, it looks great in here."

"Thanks." Massie's heart was still pounding. "What is *that*?"

"It's Derrington," Claire said, like it should have been obvious. "You didn't think you'd be practicing on me, did you?"

"No." Massie didn't know what she'd expected. "Of course not."

Claire pulled a tube of cherry ChapStick from the back pocket of her classic-cut Gap jeans and swiped it across the moose's bulbous lips.

"Ew, stop that." Massie burst out laughing. "Why didn't you take the duck or the fish? That moose's head is bigger than my leg."

"Do you really want to kiss a fish?" Claire smiled. "And duck lips are so thin and hard." She ran her finger across the dead animal's long lashes. "I thought the moose was the closest thing to Derrington." She paused and looked into his still black eyes. "Let's name him Doose, like *Derrington* and *Moose* combined."

"I get it." Massie knocked the ChapStick out of Claire's hand.

A droplet of water landed on the leg of Massie's True Religion jeans. She wiped it away, then got right back to business.

"Okay." Massie sighed. "Should we get started? The MUCK girls will be here soon."

They looked at each other and giggled. Neither knew where to begin. Massie took out her Krispy-Kreme-doughnut-flavored Glossip Girl and slathered it on her lips.

Claire held Doose at arm's length and looked him in the eyes. "Okay." She sighed. "This is how you'll be positioned seconds before the big moment. You'll be talking about something or someone and then, all of a sudden, there will be nothing left to say. And you'll just know it's time."

Massie's stomach dropped. "*What*? What do you mean I'll just *know*? What if I don't? Or what if I know and he doesn't? I need more than that, Kuh-laire."

Claire turned Doose around to face Massie. "Shhhhh, you have to relax." She shook the moose head so it seemed like he was the one talking.

Massie slapped the side of Doose's long mouth, knocking

the head out of Claire's hands. Both girls doubled over in hysterics.

"You better not do that to Derrington." Claire was still laughing.

"I might have to if I don't know what I'm doing."

Claire picked Doose up off the icy floor of the igloo and held him in front of her face. "You'll know it's the right moment, because suddenly there will be nothing left to say."

Massie felt a wave of panic crash inside of her. "No! I hate awkward silences. We get them sometimes when we're on IM and it's buh-rutal. We'll be having a good conversation and then suddenly it stops for a second and the screen is blank. Then no matter how hard I try to come up with something ah-dorable to say, it seems forced and lame and I feel like he's going to think I'm boring." For a split second Massie regretted how honest she was being. She had never been open about her insecurities beforo. It felt more uncomfortable than shower time in the OCD locker room. But at the same time, it made her feel weightless and free, a feeling she usually identified with walking down the street after Jakkob had just given her a wash and a bouncy blowout.

Claire's wide blue eyes were filled with patience and understanding. "This will be different, I promise. It won't feel like an awkward silence. It will be more like there's tons left to say, but you won't need words to say it."

Massie opened her mouth to question Claire's theory but was cut off.

"Trust me, you'll just know. You'll feel a springy tingle in your stomach."

"Okay, okay." Massie hurried her along. The MUCK girls were due any minute. "Then what?"

"Then you'll be looking at him and he'll be looking at you." Claire was gazing into Doose's black marble eyes. "And you'll inch toward each other slowly."

"Wait." Massie's hand shot up in the air like she was in class. A bead of water dropped off the roof of the igloo and slowly trickled down her wrist toward her elbow. She wiped it away without a second thought. "What if he doesn't inch and I do?"

"It's okay. Once you start, he'll follow." Claire sounded like she had been teaching courses on kissing at Harvard. "But don't close your eyes yet or you may miss your target," she warned. "Shut them slowly. Imagine they're being controlled by the dimmer switch in your bedroom."

Massie wanted to strangle Mr. Myner for having confiscated her PalmPilot. She needed to write all of this down. "Okay, so when do I close my eyes?"

"When you make contact."

"Okay." Massie sighed. She was starting to get it.

Claire handed Doose to Massie. She grabbed it with both hands and held it in front of her face. It was heavy and awkward and kept tipping to one side.

"Lemme hold him," Claire offered.

"So, you be Derrington's voice." Massie uncrossed her

legs and kneeled on her beanbag. It felt good to be the one giving the instructions again. "Say something that lets me know we're at the point where we no longer need words."

"Okay." Claire cleared her throat and hid her head behind Doose's. "I'm so glad we've been hanging out lately. I've been having a lot of fun."

Massie cracked up.

Claire glared at Massie from behind the head. "You're not supposed to laugh."

"I can't help it, I'm about to kiss a dead moose."

"That's all you'll ever kiss if you don't take this seriously," Claire snapped.

Massie was about to snap back but decided to let Claire get away with her bossy attitude. It wasn't like there were any witnesses.

"Fine." Massie repositioned Doose so that he was looking right at her. She shook her head to get back into character. "Feed me that last line again."

"Massie, I'm so glad we've been hanging out lately. I've been having a lot of fun."

"Me too." Massie stiffened her bottom lip to keep from laughing, then slowly leaned in toward Doose, her eyelids shutting with every inch she traveled. When her lips met Doose's Massie yelped and quickly pulled back. "Ow," she wailed and rubbed her top lip. "He has prickly whiskers."

Claire burst out laughing. "You want me to go get the fish?"

"Okay, okay." Massie rubbed her hands along her knees. "Give me one last pointer and then I'll just have to wing it." Massie was bored with the lesson and with letting Claire boss her around. She debated telling her she'd read William Cane's *The Art of Kissing* twice and watched his DVD. But why reveal all her secrets?

"Hmmmm." Claire looked up and rubbed her chin like she was sorting though decades of experience. "I would have to say the most important thing is to keep your lips closed. Because once you open your mouth, you're inviting a French kiss, and I'm not sure you're ready for that."

"Great, thanks, Claire." She reapplied her gloss, straightened the candles, and puffed up the beanbags. "You've been a total help," Massie admitted. She never would have thought to bring the moose.

The familiar sound of Ugg boots on twigs could be heard just outside the igloo.

"They're here." Massie fell back into the biggest, beaniest beanbag and ran her hands over her hair. This was her last chance to make the girls in her grade forget about "Nina the Obscene-a" and worship *her*. And they would. Because this time Massie was ready.

"Heyyyyy," Dylan burped when she crouched through the low entrance. She rubbed her belly. "You guys are lucky you missed the dinner. That bananas Foster was so buttery, it should come with a warning." She burped again and fanned the air around her face.

Alicia, Olivia, Carrie, Alexandra, and Livvy squeezed in and immediately made themselves comfortable.

"Welcome to MUCK." Massie tried to sound calm and confident. "Where's Layne?"

"Shesaidshehadcrampsandneededtoliedown," Carrie said. "Shemusthaveeatenthestew."

"Whatevs." Massie shrugged.

"Ehmagawd," Alicia gasped. "It looks ah-mazing in here."

"Mr. Myner is going to be so impressed," Olivia said.

"No. He. Won't." Massie sneered. "Because if he knew we were in his igloo, he would have our heads stuffed and mounted over the fireplace."

Olivia giggled at the thought.

"I'm serious, Ah-livia. He can't find out we were here."

"Don't you think he's gonna wonder where all these candles came from?" Olivia asked.

"No." Massie glared at Alicia, holding her responsible for bringing Olivia into her life. "Because when we're done, you're going to take everything back to our cabin."

"Okay, great. Now can we please get to the kissing?" Alexandra pleaded. "I am so going to smooch Kemp Hurley tonight."

"Thenyoubettertakethatchunkoflettuceoutofyourbraces," Carrie suggested.

Everyone cracked up while Alexandra used her pinky

nail to loosen the light green leaf. She reached her arm back and wiped it on the snowy wall behind her. A chunk of mushy snow fell off and plopped onto the ground.

"Ew," everyone moaned.

"*Now* do you understand why my first lesson had to be on oral hygiene?" Massie was proud of herself for making that connection. This was going to be easier than she'd thought. "So, can I assume everyone except Alexandra has been flossing and brushing?"

Everyone nodded.

"Good." Massie smiled. "Then please apply your Glossip Girl so we can get started."

All at once the girls dug into the pockets of their tight jeans. Once their lips were shiny, Massie leaned down and picked up the moose head.

"Meet Doose, our super-cute movie star boyfriend," Massie said.

The girls giggled.

"He kind of looks like Ross from *Friends*," Dylan said.

"Ithinkit'smorelikeSandraBullock," Carrie said.

Everyone cracked up.

"Okay, focus." Massie clapped her hands, then proceeded to give them the same lesson Claire had given her. She taught them to wait for the moment that didn't need words, to inch in, and to close their eyes like they were being controlled by a switch. Everyone passed Doose around and did their best despite the wiry whiskers around his lips.

"Very nicely done," Massie congratulated them.

"Now that our lips are on his, what do we do?" Livvy scraped the gloss off her lips with her teeth, then reapplied more.

"Well that's up to you," Massie said. She was very impressed by how well this was going. They were definitely looking to her for the answers, and she had them. "This is where you have to decide if you want to keep it a closed-mouther, which is fine, or if you want to take it to the next level and go for tongue." Massie avoided Claire's eyes. It was one thing to fake like you had experience but it was another to do it in front of someone who *knew* you didn't. It was like openly cheating on a test while the teacher was looking.

"Tongue." Olivia beamed. "Teach us about that."

"Ew." Livvy winced. "Can you end up with food in your mouth?"

"Only if you're kissing Alexandra," Massie joked.

Everyone laughed while Alexandra ran her fingernail across her braces. Her face was bright red.

"When using tongue," Massie became serious again, "it's important to keep it relaxed. No guy wants a stiff, pointy tongue poking around the inside of his mouth. You have to soften it and follow your partner's lead." Massie made a mental note to write author William Cane a thank you e-mail when she got back home. She'd sign Olivia Ryan's name, of course. "Everyone stick out your tongues," she insisted. "Now relax them."

They did what they were told.

"Ood." Massie responded with her tongue sticking out of her mouth. "Now move it around ut eep it re-axed."

Massie pulled her tongue in so she could speak clearly. "Now move it left, center, right, center, left, center, right, center." She clapped out the beats and they followed perfectly. "Do your best to avoid the igloo's walls or you'll get stuck." She gave them a few more minutes to practice, then told them to relax. "Those of you who want to tongue-kiss should be running these drills at least three times a day."

Livvy's hand shot up in the air. "What about those of us who just want to lip kiss?" she asked shyly.

"I suggest you put a little Vaseline on a toothbrush and scrub your lips twice a day to keep them supple. Oh, and work on holding your breath. When you're dealing with the closed-mouth variety, you've basically taken an oath not to breathe. If you do, you run the risk of being labeled a dragon, which is just as bad as having a stiff, darting tongue. So practice, practice, practice."

Carrie raised her hand.

"Yes." Massie pointed to her.

"HowlongdidyoupracticebeforeyoustartedkissingDerrington?"

"Unfortunately, I didn't have that luxury," Massie replied. "He caught me off guard and I just had to wing it."

"When exactly did this happen?" Dylan asked. "Was it at the OCD Tree-lighting Ceremony?"

"No, I bet it was after the tree-trimming gala," Alicia jumped in. "There was tons of mistletoe around."

Massie looked at Claire and then at the sheepskin rug below her feet. She hadn't prepared for these questions.

"I'd rather hear about the kisses, not the parties." Claire came to her rescue.

"Me too," Alexandra agreed.

Massie looked at Claire and thanked her with a soft half-smile. Claire gently closed her eyelids to say, "You're welcome."

"Did you go straight to tongue, or did you stay closed for a while?" Livvy asked.

"We went straight for the tongue," Massie said. "Thank Gawd he knew not to poke or dart, or I would have dumped him on the spot."

"How did *you* know?" Livvy asked.

"I have been studying the art of kissing forever," Massie said. "I've picked up some pointers from *Passions* and *One Life to Live*."

"Likewhat?" Carrie asked.

"Like always tilt your head right."

"But what if you both go right?" Olivia was confused. "Won't you bump noses?"

"No, Oh-livia." Massie rolled her eyes. "His right and your right are opposite if you're facing each other."

"Right, but what if you're *not*?" Olivia looked at the others with a cocky grin, like she had just found a big, gaping hole in Massie's theory.

Massie paused while the others laughed at Olivia's stupidity. Eventually Olivia laughed with them, but it was obvious from the flat expression behind her eyes that she had no idea why.

The drops of water started coming down a little faster now, and the girls were getting distracted. They'd have to pat their heads dry before their hair frizzed and their mascara ran.

"What'sgoingon?" Carrie asked.

"It's getting hot in herrrrrre," Alexandra sang.

Suddenly everyone broke into Nelly's old hit.

"Shhhh," Massie hissed. "We'll get busted."

"Ehmagawd." Alicia lifted her gray cashmere Ralph Lauren coat over her head. "It's pouring on me."

A steady stream of water was falling on Alicia's head.

"Turn off the heaters," Dylan yelled. "They're melting the igloo."

"And blow out the candles," Claire added.

Streams of water were pouring down all around them.

"Ehmagawd," Massie shouted. "Abort, abort!" She blew out her candles. "Everyone grab a beanbag and a rug and get out!"

"What about Doose?" Claire joked once they were all outside.

"Women and children first," Massie said.

"That lesson was killer." Alexandra shook the water off the top of her head.

"Itreallywas," Carrie agreed.

"I still want to know *when* you got all of this experience," Dylan said.

"Given," Alicia said.

At this point, Massie didn't care what they wanted. She had given them their twenty dollars' worth and was back on top. Her work here was done.

"Oh no," Livvy squealed once they were safely outside. "There are boys over there. Do you think they heard us?"

In the distance Kemp, Plovert, Cam, Josh, and Derrington were playing Hacky Sack with an ice ball under the porch light in front of the dining pavilion.

"No way, they're too far. Look." Dylan cupped her hands around her mouth and softly said, "Hey, boys!"

They all stopped and turned to face her.

"I guess sound really travels out here in the wild." She shrugged.

"What if they heard?" Alexandra said.

"Impossible, we were inside," Massie said. "Now let's get away from the igloo before Mr. Myner catches us. If he knows we melted it, he'll—"

"Hey, Block," Derrington shouted. "How about that kiss now?" The boys laughed. "Look." He pointed to the sky. "It's dark out."

Massie felt the heat of everyone's stare on her cold cheeks.

"It's not classy to do it in public," Massie shouted.

"Always an excuse." Derrington turned his back on her.

"Hey, that's not cool," Alexandra shouted. "She didn't give you an excuse at the holiday parties."

He turned back to face them.

"And she went straight to tongue," Livvy added. "You skipped right over the close-lip stage, so what are you complaining about?"

Massie appreciated the MUCK girls coming to her rescue but they needed to stop. *Now.*

"What are you *talking* about?" Derrington started walking toward them.

"Come on," Massie said to her friends. "Let's go. The last thing you girls need is to be sucked into one of our lovers' quarrels." She pulled Livvy's arm and started walking toward her cabin. Her heart was pounding and her mouth went dry. Massie suddenly felt disconnected from her body, like she was watching herself from above.

"Massie, what are they talking about?" Derrington insisted. "Have you been kissing someone else?'

Massie cringed when she heard Derrington call her by her first name. He must have been really pissed. "Keep walking," she told the girls.

"I swear, if you've been making out with some other guy while I've been waiting, I'll—" Derrington continued.

The girls stopped. "Let's go," Massie insisted.

"Whatdoeshemean*waiting*?" Carrie asked.

Derrington was standing beside them now. Clouds of steam shot out of his mouth as he fought to catch his breath.

"I want to know who you've been tongue-kissing."
Derrington looked deep into Massie's eyes.

"Just you." Massie's voice quivered.

"Me?" Derrington lifted his eyebrows. *"Ha!"*

Massie's throat got even drier as she felt the tears gathering behind her eyes.

"You mean you two have never kissed?" Alicia said. "At all?"

"She won't even let me give her a peck on the cheek." Derrington unpinned Massie's rhinestone *M* brooch from the bottom of his shorts and threw it in the dirt. He lifted his Timberland and crushed the *M* into the cold, hard ground, then turned away and stormed off.

Massie bent down to rescue her pin. She hoped a brilliant explanation for all of this would come to her before she straightened up again. But it didn't.

"I want my money back," Carrie whined. It was the first time Massie actually understood what she was saying.

"You are more fake than those designer handbags on Canal Street," Alexandra said.

"I love those bags," Olivia piped up. "They really look real, don't they?"

Alexandra glared at her.

"I am not *fake*," Massie responded deliberately. "He's lying because he's upset."

"Puh-lease," Livvy scoffed.

She turned and walked away. Carrie, Alexandra, and Olivia followed.

Dylan, Alicia, and Claire stayed behind. They stared at Massie while the others marched off in a huff. Despite the crisp night air, Massie's armpits were sweating. She was beyond humiliated and fought the desperate urge to drop to her knees and beg for forgiveness. At this point she didn't care if they revoked her alpha status forever, as long as they didn't give up on her completely.

"I know what you're thinking, and I can totally explain." Massie knew the only way she'd ever win them back was by telling the truth. But could she really admit that she felt threatened by Nina? Or that she'd been scared to kiss Derrington? Or that the thought of not being on top was more terrifying to her than pretending to be something she wasn't?

Dylan and Alicia glared at her. They shook their heads like disappointed parents and slowly walked toward her. Claire inched forward with them but looked more strained than angry, like she was holding in a poo.

Massie quickly glanced over her shoulder, hoping Mr. Myner might be nearby just in case the girls saw to it that she never moved again without the help of a full-time nurse and a wheelchair. But they were all alone . . . surrounded by miles of dense forest . . . where no one would ever hear her scream . . . or find her remains or—

All of a sudden, Massie felt Dylan's arms tighten around her torso. Her grip was so tight, Massie thought she might have punctured a lung.

"I'm so glad you were lying." Dylan bear-hugged Massie.

"What?" Massie sniffled, then wiped her eyes on Dylan's green cashmere scarf.

"I hated that you had all of this boy experience and didn't tell us."

"Me too." Alicia pouted and jumped in on their hug. "I was so sad. I totally thought we were drifting."

"Puh-lease! We're so not drifting." Massie wanted to cry with relief. "I would never make out and not tell you. I just didn't want the other girls to know our private Pretty Committee business, so I was throwing them off the trail. I thought you knew what I was doing. If I knew you believed me, I never would have—"

"Oh, puh-lease." Dylan chuckled. "We totally knew. You're just such a good actress we started falling for it."

"Yeah." Alicia widened her eyes. "You're incredible."

Claire smiled softly, shook her head, and looked out at the lake.

"I promise, I'll tell you when it happens." Massie paused and looked back at Derrington's cabin. "If it ever does."

"It will." Claire finally spoke.

"Yeah, don't worry." Dylan threw her arm around Massie. "Come on, let's go back and get changed for the bonfire reading. We'll make you look ah-mazing so Derrington will beg for your forgiveness."

"Nah, you guys go ahead." Massie smiled. "I don't feel like sitting in the cabin right now. I'll meet you at the fire pit."

"You sure?" Alicia sounded concerned.

"Totally." Massie tried to sound chipper so they wouldn't suspect that she was afraid to face the angry MUCK girls. "I just need some fresh air. It's good for the pores."

Alicia gave Massie a hug. Claire and Dylan joined in.

Massie, who was usually the first one to break away from a hug, held on to her friends as tight as she could.

Claire was the first to loosen her grip. "We'll see you at the fire pit," she said.

"Cool." Massie smiled as her friends turned to walk back to the cabin.

Massie waited until they were out of sight before making her way back. She was furious at herself but wasn't exactly sure why. Was it because she felt the need to be something she wasn't? Or was it because she was stupid enough to get caught?

She crept behind the cabin and found a lone birch tree that looked like it needed some company. Massie ran her cold palm along the soft white bark but immediately stopped when she chipped her French manicure. Couldn't *anything* go right?

She leaned against the trunk of the tree and then lowered herself until she was seated on the cold ground beneath it. Her sudden need to write was overwhelming. Massie peeled a layer of white, papery bark off the tree, pulled a purple glitter pen out of her coat pocket, and poured her heart out.

When she was done, Massie folded the bark and stuffed it in the back pocket of her jeans.

"Psssst," someone called to her from behind a nearby bush.

"Hullo?" Massie heard her own voice tremble. Were the MUCK girls spying on her? Did they have weapons? "Who's there?"

"It's me," a girl's voice answered.

"Me who?"

Massie heard a familiar phlegmy laugh. Was the trauma making her hallucinate?

"Kristen?" she whispered into the dark, cold night.

Kristen stepped out from behind the bush and giggled. She was wearing her green-and-white OCD soccer uniform.

"What are you *doing* here?" Massie hugged her friend as hard as she could.

"I used the money you gave me from MUCK to buy a ticket on Adirondack Trailways," Kristen said.

"What about all of those Presidents' Day sales?" Massie

couldn't resist a lighthearted tease.

"We already have all that stuff—it's *so* last season."

"How did you know where to find us?"

"My memory skills are incredible now," Kristen said. "I looked at your itinerary last week and the Forever Wild campgrounds address was at the top. And I remembered it."

Massie smiled and hugged Kristen again to hide her tears. It was nice to be in the company of someone who didn't know what had just happened.

"I can't believe your mom let you come here," Massie said. "She thinks *my* house is far."

"Well . . . " Kristen stuck her finger through the green Puma sweatband around her wrist. "She kinda thinks I'm away with the soccer team. So no one can know I'm here."

"I know how you feel." Massie looked over her shoulder to make sure the MUCK girls weren't spying on them.

"You do?" Kristen sounded pleasantly surprised.

Massie nodded. Kristen smiled. She could have told her friend what had happened, but why ruin the moment with more talking? Especially when they both seemed so satisfied just being together.

Massie opened her arms and threw them around Kristen.

Claire had been right: sometimes there was no need for words.

```
┌────────────────────────────────────────────┐
│                                            │
│         LAKE PLACID, NEW YORK              │
│         FOREVER WILD CAMPSITE              │
│           THE GIRLS' BUNK                  │
│         Monday, February 23rd              │
│              9:29 P.M.                     │
│                                            │
└────────────────────────────────────────────┘
```

Mr. Myner looked up from his novel, took a dramatic pause, then continued reading from *Hatchet*. "'What did they do in movies when they got stranded like this? Oh yes, the hero usually found some kind of plant that he knew was good to eat and that took care of it. Just ate the plant until he was full or used some kind of cute trap to catch an animal and cook it over a slick little fire, and pretty soon he had a full eight-course meal. The trouble, Brian thought, looking around, was that all he could see was grass and brush.'" Mr. Myner closed the book and sighed. "Powerful stuff, isn't it?"

No one said a word. They were too busy either making s'mores or blowing out the orange flames that engulfed their burning marshmallows.

"This book is full of clever ways to survive in the wild, so pay close attention," Mr. Myner said. "And you'll hear more of them tomorrow night when we check back in with poor Brian."

"I think someone left Mr. Myner in the woods when he was a kid," Layne whispered into Claire's ear.

"He wishes." Claire giggled. Their teacher was still basking in the afterglow of that last sentence, as if he were remembering the time forest nymphs sang it to him while washing his hair with spring water.

"Mr. Myner." Strawberry raised her hand. "Do we have time to make a few more s'mores?"

Her question forced his attention back to the group.

"Ten more minutes."

Everyone moaned.

"You have a long day of orienteering ahead of you tomorrow. Believe me, you'll need your sleep."

Claire stuffed two Hershey bars and a pack of graham crackers in the pocket of her light blue puffy ski jacket.

"What are you doing?" Layne asked. "I have a ton of Go-Gurt hidden under the cabin if you're hungry."

"It's not for me," Claire whispered. "It's for Massie."

"I thought she had a stomachache." Layne ran her fingers through the knots in her long brown ponytail. A clump of tangled hair came out in her hands and she tossed it in the fire.

"She does. But she may get her appetite back. And it's not like there's any food in the cabin." Claire knew better than to tell Layne the truth, that Massie was too ashamed to face her public.

"Dude, who beefed?" Plovert shouted. He fanned the air and pinched his nose shut.

"Ew, it smells like burning hair." Alicia backed away from the fire and sat on the stump beside Josh. Olivia followed her.

Smooth move, Claire thought, wishing she could just pick

up and sit beside Cam. Not that he would have even noticed. He was too busy cracking up with Strawberry, who was trying to blow out the blue flames that were scorching her marshmallow.

"Claire, stop torturing yourself," Layne insisted. "There's no way Cam would ever leave you for *that*. Trust me, there's nothing going on with them. "

Strawberry yelped as the fiery-hot marshmallow flew off the stick and landed on the side of her neck. Cam flicked the gooey clump to the ground with his index finger.

"Oh my God, he touched her," Claire gasped. "Did you see that? He totally touched her neck."

"He was just trying to help." Layne rolled her eyes.

"I have to get out of here." Claire stood up and zipped her coat pockets. She felt like she was going to faint or puke or both.

"I'll go with you." Layne scrambled to get up. "I have cramps anyway."

Claire stood up and brushed the pine needles and dead leaves off her blue flannel pajama bottoms. She quickly peered at Alicia and Josh from the corner of her eye, silently urging Josh to drop the stick he had been banging against his Timberlands so he could pay attention to Alicia. At least *that* problem would be solved. All of a sudden, Josh dropped his stick and plucked a wildflower from the ground.

Yes! Claire thought as she turned her head to give them some privacy. She was finally off the hook.

"Ready?" Claire asked Layne.

"Ready." Layne nodded once.

They turned their backs on Strawberry and Cam, who were still laughing about the stupid marshmallow, and began their short trek back to the girls' cabin.

"Hey, Claire," a guy's voice shouted. Her hands got clammy and her heart started pounding. So what if the voice didn't sound like Cam's? That didn't necessarily mean it *wasn't* him, right? Just in case, Claire made sure a big smile was on her face when she turned around. A smile that said, "I am doing just fine without you, thank you very much." Massie would have been proud.

"Wait up," the voice called again. It was Josh, holding up his roomy plaid pajama bottoms to keep them from falling down.

"Oh, this is going to be good." Layne sucked in her breath. She licked her lips and grinned, as if a big vat of Go-Gurt had just been handed to her by Chad Michael Murray.

"Maybe he's coming to tell me how much he loves Alicia."

"Doubt it," Layne said, her eyes fixed on the bluish-purple flower that was pinched between his finger and thumb.

"How cool is this?" Josh held the flower out for Claire. "It's, like, the only flower in the whole campsite."

Claire looked past his shoulder at Alicia. She was staring at them, dumbfounded, and whispering to Olivia.

"It's cute." Claire pulled Layne's arm. "Well, g'night." She turned her back to him, hoping Alicia could tell how uninterested she was.

"I got it for *you*." Josh held it out. "So you could take a picture of it or something. You know, 'cause you like taking pictures and stuff."

"Thanks, but I'm not that into photography anymore," Claire lied. "Besides, Mr. Myner took my camera so—"

"I'll take it." Layne plucked the flower from his fingers and stuck it through the elastic on her ponytail. "Thanks, Josh." She pulled Claire's arm and they were off.

"I feel so bad," Claire whispered, even though she couldn't help laughing at their abrupt exit. "I can't believe you just took the flower from him." She wiped the tears from her eyes. They felt warm against her cold cheeks. Suddenly her teeth started chattering.

"Are you really that cold?" Layne asked.

"Yeah." Claire didn't want to explain that her teeth chattered when she felt overly emotional. How was she ever going to shake the image of Cam and Strawberry laughing by the campfire?

"Claire!"

"Yeah." Claire looked at Layne as they climbed the steps to their cabin.

"What?" Layne asked.

"You just called my name," Claire said.

"Why would I call your name?" Layne said. "You're right beside me."

"Kuh-laire!"

"KUH-LAIRE!"

"Yeah," Claire whisper-yelled, trying to point her voice to

the side of the cabin, where Massie was obviously hiding out.

"C'mere," Massie whisper-yelled back. "Ah-lone."

"I better go." Claire wished she didn't have to leave Layne so soon. She was the only one who could take her mind off Cam, at least for a few seconds.

"Sounds like someone's stomachache is better." Layne opened the door of the cabin and went inside.

"Where are you?" Claire asked at full volume.

"Shhhhh," Massie hissed.

Claire knew she should have whispered. But she was scared to go behind the cabin alone at night and figured the sound of her voice might scare off any lurking beasts or escaped convicts.

"By the white tree."

Claire ran her fingers along the splintered wood of the cabin walls as she made her way toward Massie's hideout. Without a flashlight, it was her only hope of not getting her leg caught in a bear trap.

Finally Claire spotted Massie. The full moon reflected off her shiny lip gloss and helped guide Claire toward her. Massie was sitting on the ground. Her arms were wrapped around her knees and the Indian blankets from her bed were draped over her narrow shoulders.

"Why aren't you inside?" Claire lowered herself onto the frosty ground.

"I knew everyone would be back soon and I needed more

time." Massie was trying to tie a pine needle into a knot. "How was the bonfire?"

"Boring," Claire lied, knowing full well that wasn't what Massie was really asking about. "Don't worry, Derrington didn't say anything about what happened earlier."

Massie threw the pine needle over her shoulder and looked at Claire with her sad amber eyes. There was a brief moment of silence while the girls let their thoughts wander.

"The only thing you missed was Cam flirting with Strawberry." Claire flicked a stuck pebble out of the rubber grooves on the bottom of her boot. "It was pathetic."

"There's no way Cam would ever like that girl. For starters, she's, like, ten feet tall, and wide."

Claire forced herself to chuckle. "Will you please tell me your plan?" She knew she was whining but didn't care. She was desperate.

"What plan?"

"You told me you'd help me come up with a plan to get Cam back if I taught you how to kiss." Claire searched Massie's blank expression for a hint of recognition. "Remember?"

"Kind of," Massie said.

Claire's heart started to race. Was Massie trying to back out on her promise?

"Well, you have to help me first," Massie insisted. "I can't have everyone thinking I'm a lying lip virgin. I'm declaring a state of emergency."

"No way." Claire jumped to her feet. "It's my turn." She

stuffed her hands in her pockets and felt the snacks she'd stolen for Massie. The sudden urge to cry overwhelmed her. She felt stupid and taken advantage of. Again.

Claire dug what was left of her thumbnail into a piece of chocolate, pretending it was Massie's neck. It made her feel a little better, but not much.

"Okay, okay, relax," Massie relented. "Sit down."

Claire turned away. Let Massie think she was angry, not disappointed.

"Come on." Massie looked up at her with sincerity. "I'm sorry, I'm not thinking straight. I have your plan."

"You do?" Claire knew Massie was only being nice to her because she couldn't afford to make any more enemies, but she didn't care. She'd take the help any way she could get it.

"Yeah." Massie patted the cold ground until Claire sat down again. Once they were huddled under the blankets, Massie revealed her scheme.

"You need to show Cam you're serious about him," Massie said.

"But I—"

Massie held her hand in front of Claire's face and continued. "You haven't put yourself on the line yet. You haven't shown him how much you're willing to risk to get him back. You know, the way they do in the movies."

"The movies?"

"Yeah. You know, when the guy has acted like a jerk and the girl won't take him back? He always has to do something crazy to show her how serious he is. Then she forgives him. Usually he sings something stupid under her window and wakes her parents. But it always works."

"True." Claire was already trying to decide what song to sing.

"So all you need to do is sneak into the boys' cabin tonight, look Cam in the eye—either the blue or the green one, it doesn't matter—and tell him, straight up, how sorry you are." Massie looked at Claire with an expectant smile, like she was waiting for a thank-you hug or a dozen roses for her brilliance.

Claire didn't know what to say. There were so many things wrong with this plan, she didn't know where to begin. *Sneak into the boys' cabin? What if I get caught? I'd get suspended for sure. And what if Cam laughs in my face? Or ignores me, like he's been doing all week?*

"How am I going to sneak in without getting caught?"

"Easy." Massie beamed. "We'll dress you up as a boy. Mr. Dingle won't notice a thing. Have you seen his glasses? The guy is buh-lind."

"We don't even have enough girl clothes to go around. Where are we going to find boy clothes?" Claire couldn't believe she was even entertaining the thought. But it wasn't like she was willing to go through with it.

"You can borrow Kristen's soccer clothes," Massie offered.

"Kristen's?"

"She's here," Massie whispered, then shared the confidential details of Kristen's arrival. "I promise this will work. Cam still likes you: he just needs to know that you still like him."

For someone with not really any boyfriend experience, Massie seemed wise.

"How do you know all of this?" Claire asked.

Massie tapped her temple with her index finger and grinned.

Claire sighed. "Fine." She knew one thing for sure: if this didn't show Cam how much she liked him, nothing would.

Massie threw the blanket off her shoulders and sat up straight. "Now me.

"Uh . . . okay." Claire tried to shift her attention back to Massie. "You just have to act cool. You know, don't let the MUCK girls think they're right. Convince them Derrington was trying to act tough in front of his friends and then go kiss him for real."

Claire paused to read Massie's expression. Was she buying it?

Her amber eyes were squinty, like she was considering the idea but wasn't completely sold.

"Then," Claire said, as if there were more to her plan, even though there wasn't. "Thennnn . . ." She stalled until something came to her. "Then we'll arrange to have the MUCK girls walk in on you and Derrington, so they can see for themselves how wrong they were."

Massie's eyes widened and her jaw dropped. A huge smile spread across her face when she finally closed her mouth. "Love it."

Of course she did. Massie thought it was pointless to do anything unless an audience was there to witness it. And now that her first kiss could be considered "entertainment," it seemed worth doing.

"Cool." Claire couldn't believe she had given Massie good advice twice in one night. It filled her with the confidence she needed to face Cam, possibly for the last time. "Okay." Claire jumped up again. "Let's go find Kristen and her boy clothes."

Massie sighed and stood up slowly. "Let's."

"Oh, I almost forgot." Claire took the graham crackers and chocolate out of her pockets and held them out. "I swiped these for you."

Massie rubbed her shrinking stomach. "Give them to Kristen. I can't eat." She grabbed the blankets in her arms and shook out her hair. When she straightened back up, the look behind her eyes had changed. She no longer looked like a frightened squirrel. She was queen of the forest again.

Claire followed Massie to the front of the cabin, knocking branches and spiderwebs away from her face along the way.

"Ew," Massie squealed. "Look." She bent down and lifted a pair of white satin boy shorts off the ground with the end of a stick. "How *CSI* is this?"

"Those are mine!" Claire gasped.

"Double ew." Massie tossed the panties at Claire.

They flew through the air, straight toward Claire's cheek but she jumped out of the way before they touched her. "I don't mean those are *mine*, mine. I mean those *were* mine. I gave Layne and Alicia each a pair exactly like that."

"Well, one of them ditched them back here." Massie giggled.

"I have a feeling I know who it was." Claire pinched the Victoria's Secret label on the inside and lifted them off the ground.

"What are you going to do with those?" Massie covered her mouth with her hands as if she were about to puke.

"I'm going to remind Layne that tossing underwear in the woods is bad for the environment." Claire held them out in front of her and marched up the porch steps. She kicked open the door of the cabin and headed straight for Layne's bunk. Layne was sitting cross-legged on her Indian blanket, pushing her cuticles back with the bottom of her toothbrush. The minute she saw Claire coming toward her with the underwear, she slid off her bed and raced to the back of the cabin. Claire cornered her by the closets, leaving Massie alone out front to face the MUCK girls.

"Layne, you can't just throw underwear in the woods," Claire whisper-yelled. She swung the panties in front of her face. "They're not biodegradable, for starters, and—"

"I'm sorry, okay?" Layne burst into tears. "But what was I supposed to do? Give them back to you like *that*?" She ripped them away from Claire. "Or maybe I should have tossed them in the trash so Massie could find them and parade them around the boys' cabin."

"Massie would never do that."

Layne rolled her eyes, then wiped her tears with the sleeve of her pink-and-white Hello Kitty nightgown.

"She wouldn't!" Claire insisted. She didn't like that Massie was getting blamed for this when it had nothing to do with her.

"How do you know?" Layne hissed. "It's not like she's the most honest person in the world."

Suddenly Claire realized she had left Massie with the MUCK girls. If Layne felt this much resentment toward her, the others were probably tearing Massie's hair out by now.

"Look, I have to go," Claire said. She heard Layne sniffle and softened her tone. Maybe she was being a little too harsh. "Don't worry about the underwear. Just don't leave it outside."

"I'll wash it and give it back to you, I promise," Layne said. "I'll soak it in Lake Placid tomorrow morning before breakfast."

"No." Claire lifted her palm. "Please don't. I don't want them back, really."

"'Kay." Layne sniffed. "Sorry. I just don't want everyone to know I'm the first girl in the grade to get *it*."

"Don't worry, no one will know." Claire hugged Layne, then took off to rescue Massie. But from the looks of it, Massie didn't need any help.

She was standing by the fireplace with her hands on her hips, glaring down at Carrie, Livvy, and Alexandra, who were perched on a red beanbag like three bluebirds on a rock. Massie shook her head slowly, squinted her eyes, and pursed her lips. *How did she manage to turn the situation around and blame the MUCK girls?* Claire stood off to the side and watched while Massie worked.

"Well what did you *think* he'd say?" She stomped her foot. The white pom-poms on her moccasin boot bounced. "He probably felt betrayed because I told you about our most intimate moments. I'm not surprised he denied it. He was caught off guard and probably a little embarrassed."

"Sorry," Livvy squeaked.

"You should be." Massie kicked the side of their beanbag for effect.

"And now he won't even talk to me," she pouted.

Claire felt a surge of warmth fill the spaces between her ribs. She was in the presence of a true master.

"It just seemed a little weird that he completely denied *everything*," Alexandra said softly.

"Ugh." Massie huffed. "I give up." She lowered her head for a second. When she lifted it she looked utterly bored. "No wonder you three are lip virgins. You're way too immature for a relationship."

The thumping sound of Mr. Myner's heavy steel-toed boots against porch steps got everyone's attention. The girls raced to their beds and shimmied under their covers. It was five minutes past lights out.

He knocked once and then barged in before anyone told him it was okay to enter.

"Why do I still hear talking?" He smiled as he spoke,

even though he sounded kind of angry. His strong body stayed fixed under the deer head above the door frame, while his head swiveled from side to side, checking to make sure all the girls were accounted for. He wore a big cream-colored fisherman's sweater over a gray long john shirt and a pair of faded Levi's, no jacket or hat. Claire couldn't imagine why a mountain man of his proportions was teaching at a private school in Westchester. Why wasn't he living off the land and modeling on the side?

Mr. Myner's eyes stopped on Olivia. She was hanging over her bunk, whispering to Alicia but staring at Claire. When they noticed him staring, they both flopped back onto their beds. Claire's teeth started chattering. They were so onto her and Josh. She was dead.

Once the whispering stopped, Mr. Myner clasped his hands behind his back and paced across the floor. His boots left faint, muddy prints on the fluffy white sheepskin rugs, but he was too rugged to notice or care about staining the carpets. The girls, however, had been trained by their mothers and housekeepers never to wear boots in the house. And they couldn't help snickering at Mr. Myner's ignorance.

Massie kicked the bottom of Dylan's mattress. Dylan casually leaned over and bit her lower lip to prove that she too was having a hard time restraining her laughter. Massie sat up like she was doing a crunch and looked at Claire, who was in the bottom bunk beside her. Claire rolled her eyes so Massie would know that she understood why they were laughing. Of course, she never would have been clued in if she hadn't lived on the Block estate and spent ample time with Kendra Block.

"Where's Kristen?" Claire mouthed while she had Massie's attention.

Massie pointed to her mattress.

Claire's mouth fell open. Was Kristen actually under Massie's bed? She was about to lean forward and sneak a peek when Mr. Myner's booming voice broke the silence. He seemed so angry, Claire was afraid to move.

"There I was, walking the grounds, securing our site before retiring for the evening." His words sounded like the beginning of another campfire story. "When I noticed a pathetic heap of ice and snow. *Funny*, I thought. *That's exactly where my igloo was.*" He paused and scanned their faces for a reaction. But the girls gave him nothing. Claire desperately wanted to look at Massie or the MUCK girls but kept her head on the pillow and focused on the sagging mattress above her, trying not to laugh.

"So I inched closer to investigate." Mr. Myner marched over to the door and threw it open. He stepped outside, and when he returned, he was holding Doose by his antlers.

"Someone's *horn-y*," Massie whispered. Dylan, Alicia, and Claire cracked up. "And that's when I found *this*." Mr. Myner practically spit his last words. "He was buried under a pile of snow, his mouth covered in lip gloss."

Everyone's shoulders started to shake. And at the same

time, every girl in the cabin erupted into a fit of explosive laughter, except Strawberry, who had no idea what was going on.

"This is not funny," Mr. Myner snapped. "Not only did you steal lodge property . . ." He waved Doose in the air. "You destroyed *my* property. And for that you will all get up tomorrow morning at sunrise, which is at exactly . . . " He lifted his wrist to his face and pressed a silver knob on the side of his watch. It beeped three times. "Which is at exactly six-forty a.m., and you will rebuild my igloo before breakfast."

The laughter quickly transitioned into a chorus of whines, moans, and groans.

"But I didn't do *anything*," Strawberry insisted.

"Well, unless you can tell me who did, I am holding you all responsible." Mr. Myner tapped his muddy foot on the rug and waited for her to speak up.

"I-I don't know who's responsible," she said to her down-filled pillow.

"Then I will see you all bright and early at six-forty," Mr. Myner said. "Don't forget your mittens." He smirked. "It's mighty cold here in the morning."

"Cole? Co-ooole?" a singsongy voice called from outside.

"Ew." Dylan said under her breath.

Mr. Myner's expression softened. "Coming, Merri-Lee," he sang back to her.

Dylan rolled over on her side and faced the wall.

"Uh, I have to go over tomorrow's shoot schedule. So no trouble or you will be up at five to catch the first bus home." Mr. Myner gently hung Doose back on the nail above the fireplace, turned off the light, and left. No one said a word until the sound of his heavy footsteps was no longer audible.

"I am so going to puke," Dylan said. "Gawd, could she be any more desperate? Who hits on a geo teacher?"

"Desperate math teachers," Massie said. "And your mother."

Everyone giggled.

"Very funny," Dylan whined. "I swear, as soon as I'm sixteen I'm divorcing her."

While Dylan complained about her mother and Alicia and Olivia went back to whispering, Kristen silently pulled off her soccer clothes and handed them up to Massie, who discreetly passed them to Claire. It wasn't easy wiggling out of flannels and putting on sweats under a layer of heavy wool blankets, but Claire was determined. She pinned her blond hair to the back of her head and swept her short bangs to the left, because Massie insisted it drew attention to her "good side."

Once Claire was dressed, she handed her pink-and-green plaid flannel nightshirt to Massie, who tossed them under her bed for Kristen. Phase one of the plan was complete. Now all Claire had to do was stay awake until the others fell asleep. Then she would sneak out.

Somewhere between counting owl hoots and the number

of times Strawberry snored, Claire drifted off. She woke suddenly to the sound of footsteps creaking on the wood of the cabin floors. A tingle of prickly sweat welled up on the bottoms of her feet. Was it a bear? Was Mr. Myner checking up on them? Was Alicia coming to strangle her?

The cabin door opened slowly, then closed. It must be someone going to the bathroom, Claire decided. She would wait until they came back and then leave, just in case they ran into each other outside.

Sometime later—it was hard to tell exactly how much without her watch—Claire woke up again. She was mad at herself for drifting off but knew by now that whoever had been walking around was either gone or had gone back to sleep.

Claire slowly sat up in her bed. The springs squeaked a little when she moved, but no one stirred. Gently, she rose to her feet and waited to see if anyone had woken up.

Nothing.

She lifted her right leg and stretched it out as far as it would go, so that it touched one of the sheepskin rugs and not the creaky wood. When she felt the fluff beneath her wool socks, Claire took another step. She slipped on her shoes and then continued to make her way across the cabin, lightly hopping from one rug to the next, the same way she used to leap across river rocks back in Florida.

The brisk night air was invigorating. It sharpened Claire's mind and cooled the thin layer of nervous sweat that had coated her skin.

On the count of three she vowed to jump off the side of

the porch and make a run for the boys' cabin. On the count of three she would make things right with Cam. On the count of three she would risk suspension in the name of love.

One . . . two . . . three . . .

The overwhelming boy smell was a shock to her system, even though Claire should have been used to it by now. After all, it was the same musty combination of sweat and stale breath that her brother Todd's room smelled like in the morning, only ten times thicker.

Claire covered her nose with the thick, porous, polyester sleeve of Kristen's soccer jersey and breathed in the leftover traces of her friend's signature scent, Clinique's Happy. It was all she could do to keep from dry heaving.

If it hadn't been for Cam's infamous brown leather jacket hanging over the thick wood post of his bed, Claire never would have spotted him. He was curled up in a little ball, completely covered in the heavy wool Indian blankets, except for the top of his thick black hair.

Claire felt a flutter in her stomach. She had never seen Cam asleep before. She had never even seen him lying down. It was thrilling and slightly disturbing at the same time. It felt wrong to watch him when he had no idea he was being watched, like she was stealing something valuable from him.

After a deep inhale and a slow, measure exhaled, Claire decided it was time to make her move across the sock-strewn floor. She pressed her palms against the door to absorb the inevitable *click!* sound the latch would make when she shut it behind her.

There was no turning back now.

A few of the boys were snoring. The off-key blasts reminded Claire of her brother and his friend Tiny Nathan tuning up for band practice. But in this case, instead of covering her ears, Claire waited anxiously for the sounds and used them to help her reach her target undetected.

Snore . . . step . . . snore . . . step . . . snore . . . step . . . snore . . .

Claire zigzagged through a minefield of muddy Timberlands, worn messenger bags, and torn-out pages from graphic novels on her way over to Cam's bed. There wasn't a fluffy white rug in the entire cabin. And instead of a cozy beanbag-and-pillow nook by the fireplace, there were big rocks covered in plaid blankets. It was more rugged than her bunk and a lot less cozy.

Her stomach lurched as she approached Cam's bed. Would he send her away? Laugh in her face? Wake his friends up so they could all see how desperate and pathetic she was?

Someone moved on the bunk above him. Claire froze and held her breath until he settled.

Once everyone was still, Claire leaned forward and nudged Cam out of his sleep. He rolled over and faced her, then opened his blue and green eyes.

"Dude!" He shot up in bed.

Dude?

"What are you doing here?"

Claire lowered herself and sat on the edge of his mattress by his pillow.

"Sorry, I didn't mean to scare you."

"Claire?"

"Yeah."

"I thought you were Brian Jeffreys." Cam blinked a few times to clear his vision.

"Who?" Claire didn't really care what Cam was saying as long as he was talking to her.

"That girly-looking towel boy who's always begging the coach for a soccer tryout. You look exactly like him. What's with the outfit?"

Claire wanted to jump out of her skin with excitement. They were having a normal conversation. Maybe everything was fine. Maybe it had all been a bad dream.

"I need to talk to you." She twisted the green Puma sweatband around her wrist. "And Mr. Myner said that if a girl is caught the boys' cabin, she'll get sent home, so—"

"Well, if Dingle catches you here, I'll get kicked off the soccer team, so you better go." Cam flopped back down and folded his hands behind his head.

"Then let's sneak out back. I have to tell you something."

Cam didn't move. He stared at the mattress above him and breathed deeply. He wasn't going to make this easy.

"Fine." Claire stood up. "I'll leave." She stood still for a second, giving Cam one last chance to beg her so stay. But he didn't.

Claire took a deep breath and sat back down. "Look." She sighed. "I know you're mad because you saw me kiss Josh after the soccer game last week, and I totally get it."

He didn't say a word.

Claire continued. "But I thought you dumped me. You ignored me at the Love Struck dance, you never returned my e-mails, and you were all over Alicia's slutty cousin Nina. So what was I supposed to do? I was upset."

When the springs on the mattress above Cam squeaked again, Claire stopped talking. She used the quiet time to study Cam's face. His breathing remained deep and steady. If he felt any compassion, he was doing a great job of hiding it.

"Cam, I had no idea Nina told you that lie about the Spanish soccer spell. How was I supposed to know she convinced you to avoid me so you'd win the finals?"

"She told me you knew about it." Cam rolled over and faced the wall. His voice was distant and slightly muffled.

"Well, she was ahb-viously lying." Claire caught herself sounding like Massie and decided to go with it. "Puh-lease, Nina was a total klepto. She got caught stealing from everyone in school. Are you seriously going to believe her over me?"

Cam was silent.

"Cam?" Claire filled with rage.

Silence.

"Cam?"

Silence.

The more he ignored her, the more her anger swelled. Eventually, the pressure building inside her could not be contained. And all of a sudden Claire burst.

"Cam!" She smacked him on the back, hitting his bony shoulder blade. The pain, along with her pent-up frustration, brought on a swell of tears.

His back started shaking and Claire instantly forgot the throbbing in her hand. "I'm so sorry—did I hurt you?" she whisper-cried.

Finally Cam turned around to face her. He was laughing hysterically. "Even Brian Jeffreys hits harder than you."

The instant Claire saw his smile, her tears came harder. Cam had forgiven her.

His eyes sparkled with that playful flicker Claire loved, like he'd suddenly reclaimed his body and banished the cold zombie who had been living there for the last week.

Claire tried not to move. She wanted to bask in the warmth of his gaze for as long as possible, to make up for lost time. They stared at each other without blinking, until every cell in Claire's body felt electrified. She imagined her insides looked like strands of festive Christmas lights pulsing on and off, on and off, on and off, in perfect sync with her beating heart.

Even though Claire and Cam weren't speaking, their eyes, bodies, and sweat glands seemed to be communicating on a frequency all their own. They didn't need words.

Claire tilted her head slightly to the right and held it there for a second. Her heartbeat quickened and the Christmas lights flashed faster.

Slowly, Claire inched forward.

The closer she got to Cam's full lips, the more she lowered her eyelids. Even though Claire couldn't see her target, she knew she was getting closer, because the sweet smell of Drakkar Noir and Ivory soap was growing stronger. She surrendered to the feeling, allowing herself to get sucked into his invisible force field. She was falling and leaning, leaning and falling, falling and—

Finally, there was contact. Instead of landing on Cam's perfect mouth, she was facedown in a pile of itchy blankets. She threw open her eyes and gasped. Her Christmas lights went dark.

Claire kept her head buried until it became impossible to breathe. What just happened? Had she imagined the whole conversation between their bodies? Was her theory about not needing words wrong? Had Cam not forgiven her after all?

"Sorry," he said.

Claire lifted her head. She was dizzy and too embarrassed to face him. Instead, she stared at the abstract hieroglyphic pattern on his blanket until it blurred.

"What about Josh?" he asked.

"What about him?" Claire was beyond annoyed. What else did she have to do to prove she liked Cam? The soccer outfit, the pinned-back hair, sneaking over and trying to kiss him—all of this certainly should have been enough.

"He likes you now," Cam whispered. "I can't just steal his girl."

"Ew, I'm so not his girl," Claire insisted. "I wish I could take that whole thing back. I always wanted you to be my first kiss, not him. I was just hurt and—"

"Well, I want you to be *my* first kiss." Cam rested his hand on Claire's bare knee. It felt like a lightning bolt shot out of his palm and straight into her veins. But the time for their kiss had come and gone.

They needed words.

"If you want me to be your first kiss, why did you move out of the way?" Claire was shocked with herself for being so straightforward. But at this point, it was easier to ask the questions than to live with them.

"I want our first kiss to be more romantic," Cam whispered and looked around the cabin. "Not something we do in front of a bunch of sleeping guys."

"I hear you."

Yay! Romantic Cam was back.

"Besides, you look like a dude and it's kinda freaking me out."

Claire punched him in the arm and he punched her back. They both cracked up. Cam covered Claire's mouth so she wouldn't wake the guys. Before he moved it away she inhaled deeply, stealing one last whiff of Drakkar Noir for the road.

"I better go." Suddenly Claire's body ached with exhaustion.

"Meet me after dinner tomorrow night at Powwow Log," Cam whispered. "Oh, and please don't say that this is the end—I won't be happy until we've kissed."

Claire gasped. Her arms and legs immediately flared up in goose bumps. "That's the last line in the poem I sent you."

Cam pulled a folded piece of paper out from under his pillow. "I know."

"You got it?"

He smiled and waved it in front if her face as if to say, "Of course I got it, silly. And I loved it."

Claire felt like her world had just switched from black and white to Technicolor, like in *The Wizard of Oz*. She could hardly sit still.

"Just to make this the most romantic kiss in all of history, let's not speak all day tomorrow. It will be like we're a bride and groom on their wedding day," Cam suggested.

Claire's teeth started chattering. "I love that."

"Are you cold?"

"Not one bit." She beamed.

"Okay." Cam grinned. "See you at seven?"

"See you at seven." Claire stood up and smiled down at him.

Then a familiar nonboy smell filled the air. It was a spicy combination of vanilla and chocolate and . . .

It was Alicia's Angel perfume.

Was she here? Did she hear what I said about kissing Josh? No way, right? But what if she did?

Claire turned and ran out of the cabin as quickly as she could. She didn't care about creaky floorboards, waking the boys, or getting busted by Mr. Dingle. The only thing on her mind was Alicia and how vengeful she would be if she knew Claire had kissed Josh.

When she got back to her cabin Claire dove under her blankets. She was too afraid to check the beds to see if Alicia was missing. She didn't want to know. Instead she squeezed her eyes shut and prayed to God that one of those Briarwood boys had farted Angel perfume in his sleep.

"Up and at 'em, ladies." Mr. Myner burst through the cabin door and flicked on the light. The girls squinted until their eyes adjusted to the blinding brightness. He unzipped his yellow *I Know What You Did Last Summer* raincoat, revealing a pair of formfitting one-piece long johns.

It was still dark outside. And the feeling of being up before the rest of the world reminded Massie of the vacations she took with her parents to St. Barts. It was always dark when her father woke her up and urged her to "get a move on" so they wouldn't miss their early flight. No matter how much Massie had been looking forward to hitting the beach, at that exact moment, she would have forfeited her vacation just to spend a few more minutes under her warm covers with Bean.

Now that Mr. Myner was tromping around the cabin, tearing the blankets off the girls and insisting they get up, Massie had that same feeling, only worse. Because he wasn't whisking them away to a tropical island so they could sip fruit smoothies by the pool and compare iPod playlists. He was forcing them to build an igloo for him in the middle of the frozen woods before sunrise. Massie made a mental note to meet with Alicia's father about a potential lawsuit.

"Everyone on your feet." Mr. Myner clapped his hands.

Claire pushed herself off the bottom bunk and rubbed her eyes. Massie didn't know whether to laugh or scream. She was still dressed in Kristen's soccer clothes.

"Claire," Massie fake coughed. "Claire."

Claire's pale eyebrows crinkled when she looked at Massie.

Massie pointed her chin toward Claire's soccer shorts. Claire still seemed confused.

"Boy clothes," Massie coughed.

Claire's expression changed immediately, like someone had just thrown a bucket of cold water on her face. She quickly tugged a blanket off her bed and wrapped it around her like a pashmina. Massie sighed and turned back to Mr. Myner.

"Do you hear that sound?" He cupped his ear with his hand and tilted his head to the side, like he was listening to a rare birdcall.

Massie couldn't hear a thing. The rain on the wood roof blocked out all other noise. Besides, her eardrums were still asleep.

"Kind of," Strawberry lied. The pile of hair on top of her head was leaning to the left. She looked like a pink Hershey's Kiss.

"It's the sound of you getting lucky," Mr. Myner said. "It's raining, so you are off the hook. Everyone back to bed.

I'll be back after my sunrise hike to wake you." He turned off the light and, with a swish of his raincoat, disappeared into the darkness.

"My boobs have more point than that," Dylan moaned as she covered her head with a pillow.

Everyone cracked up. Seconds later, the cabin was silent. All of the girls had fallen back asleep except Massie. She was dying to know what had happened with Claire and Cam. And, more important, had Derrington been awake? Had he said anything about her? Had any of the other boys said anything about her?

Massie flipped her pillow to the cold side and lay back down. How was she was going to face another day, knowing that some of the biggest losers in the school thought *she* was a loser? The natural order of the universe had gone awry. And Massie couldn't rest until it was restored.

She quietly lifted the covers off her and slipped into her lavender angora slippers. Massie tiptoed across the floor, trying her hardest not to wake the MUCK girls. Not without a winning plan. Once she got to the fireplace, she climbed over the beanbags to the mantel. She slowly lifted Doose off his nail and did her best to lower him onto the ground without stabbing herself in the eye with his antlers. She almost had him safely on the ground when a pair of underwear fell out of the hollow part behind his snout and landed on Massie's chest.

"Ew," she whisper-yelled. Doose went crashing down onto the floor. Luckily, his fall was silenced by a cushy suede beanbag. Massie lifted him up by one antler, pinched the underwear between her thumb and index finger, and tiptoed back to the bunks.

Massie stood over Claire for a second, watching her chest rise and fall while she slept. Things must have gone well with Cam or Claire would not have looked so peaceful. Claire's love life couldn't be better than hers. She had to fix things with Derrington ASAP.

She hooked the underwear over one of Doose's antlers and lowered his face until he was nose to nose with Claire. When Claire didn't move, Massie gently poked her with Doose's hairy lips.

Her blue eyes shot open. "Ahhhhhhh!" she screamed. Massie dropped Doose on the bed and covered Claire's mouth with her hand. Everyone woke up and looked around the cabin. Massie crouched down until the girls settled back to sleep.

By then Claire's nerves had settled and the two girls buried their faces in blankets and pillows and laughed hysterically.

"What are you doing?" Claire mouthed once she caught her breath.

"Come outside, we have to talk."

"Now?" Claire hesitated.

"Yeah."

"It's raining."

"It stopped," Massie lied. "Come on, unless you want this underwear in your face." She pinched the satin panties and dangled them above Claire's nose.

"Gross." Claire slapped Massie's hand. "I'm going to kill Layne." She grabbed the underwear and dropped it on Layne's head on her way out the door.

It was raining sideways when the girls stepped out onto the porch. But the hunter green canvas awning kept them dry.

"So how did it go last night?" Massie asked, even though she already knew the answer.

"Ah-mazing," Claire said. "Your plan was perfect."

Massie smiled. That was all she wanted to hear. As far as she was concerned, they could move on to her now.

"I'm back in," Claire continued. "Cam is finally over the whole Josh thing. We're even going to have a make-up first kiss tonight at seven p.m."

"Perfect," Massie said. "Now, moving on to Derr—"

"Do you know if Alicia left the cabin last night?"

Massie shrugged. She was annoyed that Claire was still making this about *her*. It was Massie's turn to get the attention.

"Because I have a feeling she was in there when I was talking to Cam, which means she heard everything I said about Josh."

Massie shrugged again and looked out into the distance. The sun was just starting to carve out a place for itself in the overcast sky. With every passing second, Whiteface Mountain became more visible, its edges sharper, like a developing Polaroid picture. But there weren't any brilliant golds or oranges to admire. No ribbons of pink casting a warm dawn-of-the-new-day glow on Lake Placid. It was a gray, milky morning, which suited Massie just fine. She was too distraught for beauty. It would have made her feel even worse than she already did.

"Are you sure you don't know *anything* about Alicia?" Claire pressed.

"The only think I know is that I need your help," Massie hissed. "It's my turn, Kuh-laire. You promised."

"Uh, okay." Claire seemed surprised by the urgency in Massie's voice. "No problem. I just need to think for a minute."

"No need for that." Massie held up her palm. "I already have the plan all figured out."

"Oh." Claire folded her arms across her chest.

"All I need you to do is bring the MUCK girls to the tree behind the cabin tonight right after dinner. "

"Why?"

"Because that's where I'll be kissing Derrington." Massie felt a pull in her stomach when she said the words. Even though she was committed to losing her lip virginity, the idea still made her nervous. "You'll come up just as we're kissing, then I'll get mad at you for invading our privacy. Meanwhile, the girls will see us doing it and they'll apologize for calling me a liar, and Derrington and I will have done the deed and everything will go back to normal. It's perfect."

"Yeah, except for the part about you getting mad at me," Claire joked.

"Pleeeeease." Massie held her palms together in prayer.

"No problem," Claire said. "But can we do it at a different time?"

"Why?"

"Because seven p.m. is when I'm supposed to meet Cam for our kiss."

"So meet him at eight p.m.," Massie snapped. "I really need the 7 p.m. slot, because everyone will be finished with dinner and roaming around. So it will seem natural."

"But I *can't* change it with Cam," Claire insisted.

"Why nawt?" Massie stomped her angora-clad foot.

"Because Cam and I aren't speaking today," Claire said. "We're waiting until 7 p.m. It's more romantic that way."

"Kuh-laire." Massie's voice cracked. "My reputation depends on this."

Claire looked at her red socks and wiggled her toes.

"Kuh-laire?" Massie lifted Claire's head, forcing her to make eye contact. "It can't wait."

"Okay, well, hopefully Cam can," she said under her breath.

"What?" Massie asked, even though she'd heard Claire loud and clear.

"Nothing," Claire said.

"Good, then it's a plan?"

Claire opened her mouth to answer, but Massie turned on her heel and walked back into the cabin before Claire had the chance to say another word.

The usual lively lunchtime chatter was slightly muted, partly because the rain drowned out the noise but mostly because everyone was too wet to talk about anything other than how wet they were.

Claire picked the crispy bacon out of her BLT and nibbled at the crusts of the toasted sourdough bread. After a soggy morning of building shelters out of branches and bright orange tarps, she should have devoured the double-decker sandwich and the spicy fries, but her appetite was gone. How could she possibly eat when there was a chance Alicia had overheard her Josh confession? Besides, she still had to break the news to Cam that their tryst would have to wait until Massie got her social life back. And *telling* him would mean breaking their romantic vow of silence. It was all too depressing, even for a plate of hot fries.

Massie tilted her head sideways. "So what's up with Alicia and Olivia sitting over there at the boys' table?"

"I dunno." Claire was so happy to have Alicia out of the way for a while, she didn't bother questioning it.

Dylan leaned across the table and whispered to Massie. "Hey, did Kristen really spend the night under your bed?"

Massie looked around to make sure no one was listening, then nodded.

"That's worse than being buried alive." Dylan pulled a flimsy piece of mayo-covered lettuce out of her sandwich and rolled a french fry in it.

"You think?" Claire asked. "How is lying under a bed *worse* than being buried alive?" She knew she was overreacting to Dylan's comment but lately, between Alicia, Massie, Cam, and Josh, Claire felt like *she* had been buried alive, and it felt good to lash out at someone.

"Well, for starters . . ." Dylan stuffed the lettuce-fry in her mouth. "She had to spend the night lying under Massie's butt." She cracked herself up and a piece of fry shot out of her mouth and landed on her forearm.

Massie laughed too, then became serious. "We need to bring her some food. I already swiped one of Layne's Go-Gurts but she said it made her barf-burp twice. She's probably starving by now."

"And bored," Claire added. "What does she do under there all day?"

"Reads trail maps," Massie answered.

"So, what are the girly-girls talking about?" Merri-Lee sat down in the seat beside her daughter. The camera, along with its blinding light, followed.

"Mom," Dylan whined. "Do you have to get us eating?"

"What's wrong with eating?" Merri-Lee tightened the green chiffon sash around her Ralph Lauren safari jacket. Her waist was so tiny, she looked like the number 8.

"Everything." Dylan pushed her plate away and folded her arms across her chest.

The MUCK girls walked behind Dylan, looked straight into the lens, and waved. One of the nameless non-soccer team boys pushed another nameless non-soccer team boy in front of the camera, then ran away in hysterics.

"Oh, don't stop gossiping just because I showed up." Merri-Lee rolled a fresh coat of red Chanel lipstick across her puckered mouth. She snapped the cap back on and turned to her daughter. "So, what were you talking about?"

"You really want to know?" Dylan had a devilish glint in her eyes. She looked straight into the camera and smiled slowly. "We were talking about how creepy it is to watch you flirt with Mr. Myner, my geography teacher."

Claire felt her blue eyes widen. Had Dylan really just said that?

Merri-Lee smiled sweetly and put her perfectly manicured hand on her heart. "Thank you, darling." She turned to face her crew. "Okay, cut. Let's get some beauty shots of the rain on Lake Placid."

The cameraman flicked off the light and headed for the door, dragging the audio guy—who was attached to the camera by a wire—with him.

"Honestly." Merri-Lee stood up and left.

Dylan, Massie, and Claire giggled into their palms.

Then Dylan turned on the rubber heel of her pink moccasins. "I'm going to visit that little squirrel in our cabin," she said to no one in particular.

"Uh, I'll go with you." Massie stuffed a BLT in the pocket of her army green cropped bomber jacket and followed Dylan to the exit.

"Uh, I'll be there in a minute," Claire called after them, even though they didn't seem the slightest bit concerned. She sat back down at the table, desperate for a minute to herself so she could think of a way to keep things from falling apart with Cam. But it was hard with Carrie staring at her. And even harder once Alexandra, Layne, and Livvy sat down.

"What's wrong with *your* table?" Claire asked Layne.

"I knew it." Layne pulled her leopard-print earmuffs off her head and let them hang around her neck. "You're still mad about the underwear, aren't you?"

"No," Claire insisted. "I just want you to throw it out in a normal trash can."

"We moved tables because Livvy spilled her grape lemonade all over the place, and the last thing we need is more wet." Alexandra leaned back on the bench and wrung out her long, straight brown hair. Droplets of rainwater dripped onto the wood floor.

"It was an accident." Livvy scraped her top teeth across her bottom lip, obviously craving the taste of lip gloss.

Claire looked over at the boys' table. For the time being, she was more interested in spying on Alicia than Cam.

Alicia said something to Olivia and they both looked at Claire. The instant Alicia's brown eyes met hers, Claire felt her entire body stiffen. She forced herself to smile at Alicia and was relieved when Alicia waved back. And she was *smiling,* which could mean only one thing: she hadn't been there last night. She didn't know about Claire and Josh. Suddenly, Claire knew how to alert Cam to the change of plans while maintaining their vow of silence. She glared at Alicia until she looked over again and then motioned for her to come over.

Alicia stood up from the boys' table and glided across the room. She swayed her hips back and forth with every slow step she took. Her tight navy blue stretch corduroy Sevens hugged her perky butt and accentuated her sexy saunter. If Alicia knew the boys were staring at her, she did a good job of hiding it.

"Hey, what's up?" She stopped and stood over Claire, nothing but sweetness in her voice.

Claire searched for signs of insincerity before continuing. But Alicia's brown eyes twinkled with warmth and kindness. The only thing Claire found suspect was how well Alicia's good looks held up in the rain.

"Is this about Dylan?" Alicia seemed genuinely concerned. "Is she upset because Olivia and Plovert are hanging out? I mean, I know they went to the Love Struck dance together, but Dylan swore she wasn't into him because he smelled like fake tan." She was speaking faster than usual, and it made Claire a little nervous. "Tell me the truth, is that why she left?"

Claire stood up and faced Alicia. She didn't want the MUCK girls eavesdropping on their conversation. "No, she hasn't thought about Plovert since her mother got here. She left to bring food to Kristen."

"Oh, cool." Alicia turned back to Olivia and gave her the thumbs-up. "So what's up?"

"I was wondering if you could deliver a note to Cam for me." Claire shifted her weight from one leg to the other.

"Given." Alicia pulled out a tube of peach-colored Nars lip gloss and rubbed the wand across her lips while Claire wrote on a napkin.

C,
Something came up. Can we meet at Powwow Log at 7:30 p.m. instead of 7 p.m.? If it's cool, ignore me. If it isn't, send a note. Can't wait.
C

Claire folded the napkin into a small, tight square and pressed it into Alicia's palm. She watched Alicia stroll back to the boys' table and waited for her to signal that Cam had gotten the note. Once she got the confirmation nod, Claire sat down and dug into her BLT. All of a sudden she was ravenous.

"Rate me out of ten," Massie commanded Claire as they hurried up the steps of the shower house. The rain had finally stopped but the ground was still moist. The air smelled like a mix of fresh-cut grass and wet poodles.

"Ten."

"You're just saying that." Massie pulled up the straps of her emerald green satin cami and tightened the knot on her short, cream-colored cashmere tie-front cardigan.

"I am not. You look ah-mazing." Claire looked over her shoulder, probably checking for Mr. Myner. "Those new True Religion jeans look great on you."

"They're Alicia's." Massie rolled her eyes.

She clearly missed her conditioner-soaked wardrobe, which had arrived safely at Westchester's Delicate Dry Cleaners yesterday morning, thanks to FedEx.

"Well, you should ask her if you can keep them," Claire suggested. "They look great on you."

"Thanks." Massie pulled open the door to the shower house and looked over her shoulder to make sure they weren't being followed.

If Mr. Myner caught them sneaking out of dinner early, the Lumber-Jerk, as Massie had dubbed him, would find some psychotic way to punish them. Maybe this time he'd wake them up at 3 a.m. to dust the leaves on the spruce trees.

"Kuh-laire, tens are reserved for special occasions only." Massie held the door open for Claire. "If you start giving out tens on normal days, what are you going to give for parties or proms? Where do you go from there?"

"Fine, you're a nine." Claire sighed.

"Really?" Massie raced over to the wide mirrors that covered the walls by the marble-topped dressing stations. "What could I do to be a ten?" she asked her reflection.

"You could relax." Claire batted her short French-girl bangs from one side to the other. "Ugh, I can't believe it's the eve of my first kiss with Cam and I look like *this.*"

Massie felt an anger surge zip through her body. "Claire, were your parents lobsters?"

"Uh, no." Claire pinched her cheeks until they were rosy.

"Then why are you acting so shellfish?" Massie said.

"What?"

"Kuh-laire, in exactly . . ." Massie checked her wrist, then slammed it against her thigh when she realized the Lumber-Jerk had confiscated her Coach watch. "In about ten minutes I will lose my lip virginity. You, on the other hand, have already lost yours, no matter how much you and Cam want to pretend you didn't. So can we please stay focused on me right now?"

"Sorry." Claire stuffed her Cover Girl lip gloss in the back pocket of her Gap classic-cut jeans.

"I can't believe you never kissed Derrington," said an echoey voice from one of the shower stalls.

Massie's body froze. She was so nervous about her kiss, she'd forgotten to check to see if anyone was there. How could she have been so careless?

"It's just me." The voice was followed by a familiar phlegmy laugh.

"What are you doing in here?"

Kristen padded barefoot into the changing area. Her body was wrapped in a thick green Turkish cotton bath towel and her short wet hair was spiky and wild. "BTW, how much do you love these heated tile floors? I don't even need slippers."

"Kristen." Massie stomped her foot. "What are you doing in here?"

"I should ask *you* the same question." Kristen pulled a Q-tip out of the glass jar by the mirror. Her mouth hung open and her eyes glazed over while she twirled it around the inside of her ear. "Dinner isn't over until seven." She smiled proudly. "I memorized your schedule. I also studied all of the trail maps and have managed to commit most of the bird and animal species to memory."

Massie rolled her eyes. She was so over listening to everyone else's problems. She had major issues and no one seemed to care.

"I'm so bored." Kristen opened a jar filled with blue water. She stuck her hand inside and pulled out a black comb, tapped it on the side of the glass, and combed back her short hair. "This place has everything. I would never want to leave if I didn't have to spend all of my time hiding under a bed eating Go-Gurt and leftovers."

"Yeah, that sucks." Massie tried to sound sympathetic, but all she could think about was Derrington and how far over to the right she should tilt her head before the kiss.

"The worst part is, there isn't a bus out of here until tomorrow night." Kristen sighed at her reflection.

"So?" Massie felt her jaw tighten. She desperately wanted to tell Kristen to shut up so she could think clearly but fought the urge with every bit of strength she had. After all, the girl had spent the last two days lying on a wood floor and probably needed a minute to vent.

"I can't just show up at home early." Kristen turned away from the mirror and looked at Massie like she was insane. "My parents aren't expecting me back until Friday."

"Tell them the soccer game got canceled because some-one got hurt," Claire suggested.

Ugh! Why is everyone so obsessed with Kristen and her lame parents? Can we puh-lease move on?

Massie felt the anger building inside her again. It came harder and faster than it had before. Even the roots of her hair ached from the pressure. She couldn't hold it in any longer.

"Kuh-risten." Massie turned away from the mirror and looked her friend directly in the eye. "Puh-lease! I am trying to get myself into game mode here and I can't if you keep going on about your ahn-noying parents and your stupid memory skills. Try to think about someone other than your-self for once."

Kristen's green eyes immediately welled up with tears.

"Suh-orry." Kristen gathered her clothes and stomped barefoot toward the door. "But I was under the impression that you and Derrington *already* kissed. Re-mem-ber?"

"I know. I'm sorry I lied." Massie felt terrible for making her friend upset. She wanted to explain everything but would have wait. The clock was ticking.

"Whatevs." Kristen hurried out.

"So what are you going to tell the MUCK girls?" Massie asked Claire once she heard the door slam.

Claire was too stunned to answer. She was still focused on Kristen and her tears, but once again, Massie didn't have time to worry about that. Not tonight. Why couldn't anyone understand that?

"Kuh-laire." Massie slammed her plastic tube of vanilla-flavored dental floss down on the marble countertop. She was so frustrated she wanted to cry. "What are you going to tell the girls?"

"Uh." Claire stopped picking her cuticles and looked up at Massie. "Okay, sorry." She cleared her throat and stood up tall. "I'm gonna to tell them I saw you and Derrington sneak off behind the girls' cabin and that we should go spy on you."

"And you're sure you can get them there quickly?" Massie started pacing.

"Positive." Claire nodded.

The gentle sound of the lake lapping up against the sandy strip of narrow beach was suddenly drowned out by the noise of everyone piling out of the dining pavilion. Dinner was over and free time had officially kicked in. Everyone had forty-five minutes to do whatever they wanted before Mr. Myner continued his fireside reading of *Hatchet*.

Massie inhaled and held her breath for as long as she possibly could. When she exhaled, her tensed shoulders finally relaxed.

"You're a sex goddess in three . . . two . . . one," she told herself. When her countdown was over, she lifted her head and dabbed on a final coat of Cinnabon Glossip Girl, making sure the center of her bottom lip had an extra dollop, to make it look fuller. "Okay, let's do this."

The weight of the thick gloss on her mouth made her feel secure and safe, like she was wearing a protective shell. "I'm going to get Derrington. As soon as you see us behind the cabin, get the girls."

"Got it." Claire turned toward the mirror and fussed with her short bangs.

Massie rolled her eyes and threw open the door of the shower house.

I swear, Massie thought to herself as she made her way down the steps of the shower house, *if Claire messes this up because she's too focused on her Cam kiss, she will be dead to me.*

There was a damp chill in the air and Massie jammed her hands into the side pockets of her black satin bomber jacket to keep warm. Her knuckle brushed up against one of the sharp points of her *M* pin and scraped her skin. She had forgotten it was in there. All of a sudden she flashed back to the humiliating moment when Derrington had ripped it off his shorts and tossed it in the mud. The memory was enough to make her want to back out of the plan and hop on the next Adirondack Trailways bus with Kristen. What if he was so mad at her he refused to go behind the cabin? What if Claire brought the girls over and he was yelling at her? What if he really didn't like her anymore? How long would it take for her to get over him? Would she act as pathetic as Claire, or would she handle heartbreak with grace and dignity? Massie shook that thought from her head, hoping she'd never be in the position to find out.

She stepped away from the light of the shower house and hid in the shadows, watching her friends flirt and giggle outside the dining pavilion.

Olivia and Alicia were taking turns trying to walk using Plovert's crutches while Josh held him up to keep him from falling. Kemp and Derrington were trying to convince Dylan and the MUCK girls to eat leaves, Layne was playing Hacky Sack with the nonsoccer boys, and Cam was walking toward Powwow Log with a huge smile on his face. Massie felt like an outsider, a pathetic wannabe. And that was unacceptable.

She stepped out of the darkness and took long, confident strides toward Derrington without looking back.

"Hey, Livvy's gonna eat a twig for twenty dollars," Dylan announced when Massie joined their circle.

"Great." Massie reached for Derrington's hand and pulled him away without saying another word.

"What are you doing?" Derrington shook his arm free and stopped halfway between his friends and the girls' cabin. His voice was more serious than Massie had ever heard it before. Normally he would have been a lot more playful, but he was clearly confused, maybe even a little frightened.

"I *have* to talk to you," Massie insisted. She tried to make it sound urgent, so even if he were mad at her, his curiosity would compel him to follow her.

"Oh, *now* you want to talk to me?"

"What's that supposed to mean?" Massie asked, even though she knew. She remembered her too-nauseated-to-talk performance on the bus and all the other times she'd avoided being alone with Derrington since they had arrived at the camp. "Where are you taking me?"

"I'd like a little privacy," Massie purred, throwing in a sex goddess wink for good measure. Where were the MUCK girls? Why hadn't they seen *that*?

"Fine." Derrington's expression softened. He held out his arm so Massie could grab it again. She didn't let go until they got to her birch behind the girls' cabin.

Massie leaned against the tree and positioned Derrington so he faced her. That way the girls would see her front and center when they approached.

"What?" He hooked his fingers through the belt loops on his khaki shorts and rocked back and forth on the heels of his Timberlands.

Massie had no idea what to say next. She thought about explaining why she'd been ignoring him and considered apologizing for lying to the MUCK girls about their kissing history. But nothing seemed appropriate. Derrington looked too ah-dorable for a serious conversation. He was bobbing his head up and down to a mysterious beat that must have been playing in his head and only stopped when he heard the boys laughing in the distance.

"Wonder what happened." Derrington's dirty blond hair blew around his sparkling brown eyes. He looked like an anxious puppy dog that wanted to be let out to play.

Was this the moment Claire had been talking about? It had to have been, because Massie had no clue what to say next. *You're going to have your first kiss in three . . . two . . one,* she told herself. Then she tilted her head a little to the right.

"What?" Derrington asked.

"What what?" Massie repeated, her head still cocked.

"You look confused," he said.

She lifted her head a little, realizing she might have tilted it a little too far, giving him the wrong idea.

"I'm not confused," Massie said softly. "Au contraire." She lowered her eyelids until Derrington's face blurred. Then, slowly, ever so slowly, she moved toward him. Massie stuck her hand inside her coat pocket and squeezed her *M* pin. The sharp points hurt as they dug into her palm, but the pain gave her something to focus on other than her pounding heartbeat and sweaty pits. She squeezed the pin harder.

Think of the dimmer switch in your bedroom.
Think of the dimmer switch in your bedroom.
Think of the dimmer switch in your bedroom.

Massie thought she heard Derrington giggle and opened her eyes. But his mouth was soft and relaxed, almost like he was asleep. As she got closer to his face, Massie felt the warm tickle of his breath above her lip. She was in his airspace and milliseconds away from touchdown.

Where was Claire?

But girls or no girls, Massie couldn't stop. She was in too deep. And to pull back now would be like asking someone to stop diving once they'd already jumped off the board.

Finally their lips touched. And then they pressed together. With every passing second the pressure got stronger, until Massie's top teeth felt like they were being forced to the back of her skull. But she didn't mind. It still felt better than kissing Doose. At least Derrington didn't have whiskers.

Massie released her grip on the *M* pin and slowly slid her hands out of her pocket. She placed them gently on Derrington's hips, like they were slow dancing. He hooked his fingers through her belt loops and rocked back and forth to the beat of whatever was playing in his head.

Where's Claire?

Massie felt like her head was going to explode from lack of oxygen and didn't know how much longer she could hold her breath.

Hurry, Kuh-laire.

Right when Massie thought she was going to pass out, Derrington pulled away and gasped for air. Massie searched his face for signs of extreme joy. She longed to see a loving glint in his eye or a satisfied smile on his face. But all she saw was the back of his palm wiping the shiny Cinnabon gloss off his lips.

Did I do it wrong? Was the Cinnabon flavor too sweet? Would something in a traditional mint have been better? It's all Claire's fault for teaching me to kiss on a stupid moose.

Massie looked over Derrington's shoulder but no one was there. Now they would have to kiss all over again. But that didn't seem so terrible. She was actually looking forward to it. Massie tilted her head again and slowly leaned forward. But Derrington stepped away.

"Block." His voice was shaky.

"Yeah." Massie batted her eyelashes. She wanted to look pretty and girly when he said, "I love you."

"I . . ." He paused and looked down at his boot. He gently kicked the side of the tree a few times before continuing. "I, uh—"

"What is it?" Massie tried to sound patient but needed him to say it before the girls showed up so she could kiss him again.

"I, uh, don't think we should hang out anymore."

"What?"

Massie heard a loud ringing in her head. Everything around her started spinning and her mouth tasted like pennies. Was this really happening? Maybe they were still kissing and the lack of oxygen to her brain was causing her to hallucinate.

"You're just so moody," Derrington said. "I never know—"

Massie heard footsteps crunching in the leaves. They were getting louder and closer. It was Claire and the girls. Without another thought she grabbed Derrington's head. She skipped the head tilt, the dimming eyes, and the gentle touchdown and went straight for his lips.

Derrington was so surprised, he lost his balance and fell back into the snow. Massie knew his bare legs must have been numb but decided to worry about that later, once the audience had cleared out.

The MUCK girls were *shhh*-ing one another and giggling. Massie only had one option. She threw herself on top of Derrington and continued to kiss him on the lips. The more he struggled, the harder she pressed into him. And when she couldn't hold him in position any longer, Massie lifted her head and looked past Derrington. She widened her amber eyes and opened her mouth, hoping the girls could make out her horrified expression in such low lighting.

"Kuh-laire," Massie screeched. "What are you doing here? Can't I get any privacy?"

The girls ran off immediately, leaving Claire behind to face Massie alone.

"Sorry." Claire tried to sound regretful.

"Just leave." Massie winked.

Once everyone was gone, Massie stood up. She felt light and giddy. She held out her hand and lifted Derrington to his feet. The backs of his bare legs were red. But all Massie could think about was the look of shock on everyone's faces when they'd seen her on top of him. Her plan had worked perfectly.

"Sorry." Massie fluffed her hair. "They can be so immature."

Derrington didn't say a word. He was too busy rubbing the backs of his knees.

Massie wondered if he still meant what he had said about them not hanging out anymore. Maybe he'd changed his mind. Now that they'd gotten kissing out of the way, she had no reason to avoid him anymore. In fact, now she wanted to see him all the time.

"So, uh, why'd you do that?" Derrington tugged on one of the tree branches that hung above his head.

"I . . ." She paused. It wasn't like she could just come right out and say, "I needed to kiss you to get my popularity back." And now that it was over, Massie wasn't even sure that was the only reason she'd done it. She actually liked kissing Derrington.

"Well?"

"I wish you would change your mind," Massie whispered in case any of the girls were still listening.

"Why?" Derrington asked. "It's not like you like me or anything."

"That's so un . . ." Massie stomped her foot.

"Un-*what*?" He tore a leaf in half.

"Untrue." Massie's voice cracked. "It's *you* who doesn't like *me*, remember?" This was not the conversation she'd expected to have after her first kiss and suddenly, Claire's do-over obsession with Cam started to make sense. It sucked when things didn't go as planned, especially first kisses.

"Why do you say *that*?" Derrington crumpled up the leaf and threw it on the ground.

This was getting ahn-noying. "Be-cause you said you didn't want to hang out anymore."

"Oh." Derrington looked at Massie for what seemed like the first time. His expression softened and his eyes lit up. "That was before."

"Before we kissed?" Massie felt funny saying *kissed* out loud. It was kind of embarrassing.

Derrington turned red. "No, before I knew you liked me."

Massie crinkled her eyebrows, grateful for the wax she'd gotten just before the trip.

"I just said those things because I thought you were going to say them to me first." Derrington bit down on his lower lip. "I thought you were over me."

"No," Massie said. "I just wanted our relationship to be private. You know how much I hate being in the public eye. It can be so ahn-noying sometimes."

Massie reached into her pocket and pulled out the *M* pin. "Want this back?" She tilted it back and forth like a hologram, so he could see the rhinestones glisten in the moonlight.

Derrington held out his hand and wiggled his butt. He closed his fist around the pin, then fastened it to the bottom of his shorts.

Then, without saying a word, he leaned in and gave Massie a long thank-you kiss. It felt so good, Massie decided to keep this one to herself.

The minute the MUCK girls saw Massie lying on top of Derrington, Claire knew her mission was accomplished. She was free to meet Cam.

Finally!

She had a zillion questions for Massie, including, *What were you and Derrington doing on the ground? Did you like your first kiss? Were you nervous? And was my timing okay?* But all of that would have to wait until later. She had waited weeks to kiss Cam, and now that their time had come, Claire wasn't going to let anything stand in her way. Not even Massie Block.

Everyone was indoors now, changing into pajamas for the nighttime reading. Except for Mr. Myner and Mr. Dingle, who were tossing logs and leaves into the pit so the fire would be in full blaze when everyone arrived. Merri-Lee was perched on one of the logs beside them, sipping a glass of white wine.

"Everything okay, Claire?" Mr. Myner crouched down and snapped a branch across his manly kneecap. He chucked both halves into the smoldering pit.

"Yup," Claire chirped as she passed them. She knew she

should have stopped but it was almost impossible. There was too much energy coursing through her body.

"Then where are you racing off to?" Mr. Myner asked. "Evening program starts in fifteen minutes."

"Oh, uh, yeah, I know." Claire smiled. "I just forgot my gloves in the dining pavilion and I wanted to get them."

"Would you like an escort? It's a little dark over there."

The bottoms of Claire's feet tingled. In a few seconds she would be alone with Cam, surrounded by darkness. The idea was thrilling and terrifying at the same time, like riding a giant upside-down roller coaster.

"No, I'm fine." Claire hurried farther ahead before he could insist on joining her. "I know exactly where they are."

"Okay, just holler if you need backup." He smiled like a fearless superhero.

"'Kay," Claire shouted over her shoulder.

"You're so brave, Cole." Merri-Lee giggled.

"Ew," Claire said to herself. Dylan's mother flirting with their geography teacher was more disgusting than Layne licking the rim of an empty Go-Gurt tube.

Once she was out of their view, Claire forced herself to slow down. She didn't want to show up all panting and sweaty. Besides, it was better to appear casual and confident. Claire leaned back against the shellacked wood walls of the dining pavilion and applied a fresh coat of cherry-flavored ChapStick to her lips. After a quick bang fluff and a few cheek pinches, she was ready.

She made her way across the grass toward Powwow Log taking light, graceful steps. She wanted to appear before Cam like a beautiful angel. Not like a desperate sex maniac. She tried to steady her breathing by holding her breath as long as she could, then exhaling through her nose, a little bit at a time.

The closer she got, the more Claire was certain that they had picked the perfect spot. The log faced Lake Placid and was lit by the silver light of the moon as it reflected off the water's glassy surface. It was the best seat in the house.

Claire, now only a few feet away, was able to make out Cam's silhouette. She felt the urge to run again but somehow managed to control herself. Cam's torso looked a little wider than usual and Claire assumed he was hunched over, trying to stay warm. As she got closer, she heard his soft voice. She smiled. He was talking to himself. Knowing Cam, he was rehearsing a romantic poem he had written just for her.

"I've been wanting to do this for a long time," Claire heard a girl say.

"You have?" Cam sounded surprised.

"Uh-huh." The girl inched closer and slowly leaned in toward him.

He made no effort to push her away.

Every muscle in Claire's body tensed up except her heart. It pumped faster than it ever had before, like it was about to burst through her chest and pummel the slutbag who was moving in on her guy. And Claire was more than happy to step aside and let it.

"Cam, stop! What are you doing?" Claire didn't care how desperate the outburst made her look, or who heard.

Cam whipped his head around and jumped to his feet. The girl stood up slowly, staying close to his side. The moonlight shone at their backs, making it almost impossible to see their faces. But Claire assumed it was Strawberry. Who else could it be?

But when the girl turned to face Claire, she recognized her silhouette immediately: the thick, full hair . . . the thin frame . . . the big boobs . . .

"Alicia?" Claire whispered softly.

"Given." She didn't seem the least bit sorry.

"Is this your way of getting back at me?" Claire wasn't exactly sure who the question was directed at. It could easily have applied to both of them.

"Now you know how I feel." Alicia put her hands on her hips, letting beams of light through the spaces between her arms. The dramatic lighting made her look like an evil sorceress.

"What?"

"You kissed Josh when you knew I liked him," Alicia said. "And now you know how it feels."

"Wait, you were using me?" Cam asked Alicia. He sounded slightly hurt.

Both girls ignored him.

"Alicia, I never would have kissed Josh if I thought you still liked him. You told me at the game that you were over him." Claire could hear her voice trembling. "Besides, I don't even like him. I never did."

"Well, I don't like Cam, but that doesn't make you feel any better, does it?" Alicia said.

"Thanks a lot." Cam ran his hands through his wavy black hair and stepped away from Alicia.

Claire was torn between wanting to comfort him and wanting to kick him in the neck.

"Why did you go along with this?" Claire shifted her anger to Cam. "Was this your way of getting revenge too? Because kissing Josh was a mistake, okay? A mistake! I'm sorry. What else do I have to do to prove it?" Tears flooded Claire's blue eyes. She blinked them back but they fell forward and spilled down her cheeks anyway.

"Me, out for revenge?" Cam took a step toward Claire. "I thought *you* were out for revenge."

She stepped back. "Me? Why?"

"Because you never showed up tonight." Cam lowered his voice. He no longer sounded angry. It was worse than that. He sounded heartbroken.

"What are you talking about?" Claire's voice sounded higher than usual. "I gave Alicia a note to give to you. It said I'd be late."

No one said a word. It was suddenly very clear what had happened.

"Ooops." Alicia covered her mouth with the palm of her hand. "I must have forgotten to deliver it. My bad." She skipped toward the bushes and met up with Olivia, who had been crouched down and hiding behind a pine tree. The girls burst out laughing and speed walked toward the cabin, because Alicia refused to run.

"Claire, I'm sorry." Cam took another step toward her. "Nothing happened. It was a big misunderstanding."

But Claire didn't want to hear his excuses. She knew what she'd seen and couldn't bear to look at him anymore.

"Where are you going?" Cam called after her.

The rhythm of her footsteps on the ground along with the jagged breaths she took in between sobs formed a melodic beat that gave Claire something to focus on besides the desperation in Cam's voice.

Claire hid along the side of her cabin and waited for her tears to stop. She thought about splashing water on her face in the shower house but knew it would probably be full of girls getting ready for the evening program, and she didn't feel like explaining the reason for her tears. In fact, she wished someone would explain it to her. The more Claire thought about it, the more the situation reminded her of what she'd done with Josh. She'd given in to his advances because she'd been hurt by Cam and had wanted to feel loved. And technically, that was what Cam had been doing with Alicia. He'd thought Claire had blown him off. He'd been hurt and vulnerable and . . .

A piece of white satin buried under a pile of dirt suddenly caught Claire's attention. She kicked the leaves aside and found her underwear, once again. Only this time, the discovery made her burst out laughing. At this point, what else could she do?

Claire cautiously opened the door to her cabin and peeked inside. Was Alicia in there waiting for her? Was she updating the girls on what had happened? Were they going to laugh at her?

But no one even noticed Claire when she finally stepped inside. Everyone was crammed together on Massie's bed, applying a green mud mask to Doose's face and recounting the details of her horizontal lip kiss for the unfortunate girls who'd missed it.

Claire made it to the back of the cabin unnoticed and changed into her plaid flannel pajamas. She breathed a sigh of relief once she realized Alicia and Olivia were not there.

Claire and Layne sat in the very back of the group during the evening bonfire. From there Claire could catch glimpses of Cam, who looked down the whole night and played with the zipper on his leather jacket. Alicia and Olivia sat as far away from him as possible, pretending to listen to Mr. Myner read from *Hatchet*, but they were really more focused on braiding each other's hair. Massie sat beside Derrington and giggled while the MUCK girls studied her every move.

Claire couldn't wait to crawl under her covers and disappear for the next ten hours.

When bedtime finally came, everyone fell fast asleep. The cool fresh air and the long, active day had made it almost impossible to stay awake. Claire's body felt heavy and sore from crying all night, and the minute she hit the goose-down pillow, she melted into its fluffy embrace.

A few moments later, she opened her eyes and looked around. It was still dark outside, and in the fog of sleep she wondered what she was doing awake.

"Claire," whispered a girl. She was sitting on the edge of Claire's bed wearing shiny lip gloss that smelled like doughnuts, black eyeliner, and tons of red blush. Her wavy hair was pinned off her face with rhinestone barrettes and a short, cream-colored cashmere tie front cardigan hung around her broad shoulders, leaving the rest of her naked torso exposed. Claire sat up and looked around to see if anyone else saw what she did.

"Shhh, it's me," said the girl. That was when Claire noticed her eyes. One was green and the other was blue.

"Cam?" Claire whispered.

"Call me Camille," he said in falsetto.

Claire giggled. He looked like a transvestite version of Massie. The thought of this ah-dorably handsome soccer star applying lip gloss in front of the mirror made staying mad impossible. He'd obviously gone to Massie and poured his heart out or she never would have lent him her precious tie-front cardigan. And here he was, dressed as a girl, risking his pride and his position on the soccer team just for her.

"Here." Cam pulled a clear bag filled with gummy feet and sours out of his demin miniskirt pocket.

"Where did you get these?" Claire wanted to throw her arms around him. It had been weeks since he'd brought her candy. She untied the knot on the plastic bag and dug into it.

"I brought them from home and hid them under my mattress," Cam said shyly. "You know, just in case we made up."

"So you wanted to make up too?"

Cam nodded and smiled brightly, unable to play it cool.

"Then why were you ignoring me?" Claire smacked him playfully on the arm.

"Because I wasn't sure if you liked Josh," Cam said. "You know, until some dude showed up in my cabin and set me straight."

Once again, Massie Block had been right.

Claire pulled out a red sour and popped it in her mouth. Then she took out an orange foot and fed it to him. They watched each other chew with huge grins on their faces. Once they swallowed, Cam wiped his glossy lips on the back of his hand, then tilted his head to the right. Claire did the same. And without hesitation they leaned in toward each other.

Cam's lips were soft and full and sweet. His kiss didn't feel cold and foreign like Josh's had. It felt more like trying on a pair of jeans and realizing they were made just for her.

The longer their lips touched the hotter Claire's cheeks became, until she found herself wondering how much longer she could kiss before her head exploded.

Finally Cam came up for air. "I better go before I get kicked off the soccer team."

"Okay," Claire tried to say but no sound came out of her mouth. All she could do was watch him walk away in Massie's moccasin boots and giggle.

Her first kiss with Cam was nothing like she'd imagined it would be.

It was much better. And well worth the wait.

"Can someone please pass the butter?" Claire refused to ask Alicia, even though the silver tray was right next to her plate.

Alicia ignored her and continued dumping ketchup on her egg whites.

"The butter, please," Claire insisted.

Alicia poured herself a glass of fresh-squeezed orange juice. "Want some?" she asked Olivia, who was seated beside her.

"Sure." Olivia smiled and held out her glass.

Claire stood up and stomped to the other side of the table. She leaned over Alicia's shoulder and grabbed the butter tray. The bell sleeve of her gray J.Crew cowl-neck sweater brushed against Alicia's cheek. She didn't apologize.

Claire moved with a confidence Massie had never seen before. Her chin was lifted, her shoulders back, and she had a fearless look in her eyes, like she was being protected by some invisible force field that let her act however she wanted.

"Kuh-laire, what's going on?" Massie whispered in Claire's ear once she was seated. "You're acting so un-Claire-ish."

Claire beamed. "We did it last night."

"You did?" Massie forced herself to smile. She was happy for Claire but couldn't help wondering why she hadn't been told the big news right after it happened. Was she the first to know or was Layne? Who else had Claire told before her?

"Uh, should I keep it a secret?" Massie widened her amber eyes, hoping the innocent expression masked her true feelings. "Or does everyone know?"

"No one knows yet." Claire took a sip of grape juice.

Massie sighed. "That's so awesome." She smiled for real this time. "Tell me everything. Don't leave one thing out."

While Claire recounted Cam's romantic late-night visit as Camille, Massie placed the hunter green cloth napkin on her lap and lifted her silver knife and fork. In one swift movement she sliced through her eggs Benedict. The bright yellow yolks cascaded over the crispy ham, spilled off the toasted English muffin, and dripped onto her white china plate. It reminded her of the paint-splattered Jackson Pollock paintings in Alicia's house. She stabbed the cut piece with her fork and stuffed it in her mouth, grateful to have her appetite back. Her clothes were starting to sag in all the wrong places.

She lifted the green napkin to her mouth and dabbed at the corners of her lips, trying her hardest not to wipe off her lucky Cinnabon gloss in the process. Derrington was at the table beside hers, flinging a knifeful of grape jelly at Kemp. Massie quickly turned away before he caught her checking him out. How long would it be before they kissed again? Would they start doing it in the day? Or would it stay an après-dinner thing? And what would happen when they got back to Westchester? Massie's stomach locked up again and she pushed her plate to the side.

"It looks like everyone around here is getting action except for me." Dylan twisted her long red curls into a chignon at the nape of her neck.

Claire turned red when she realized Dylan had heard everything she'd said about Cam. "I was totally going to tell you."

"It's not that." Dylan leaned across the table so that she was face-to-face with Claire and Massie. "It's just that I've been so stressed about my mom and Mr. Myner that I haven't had any time to devote to my crush on Chris Plovert."

"So?" Massie shrugged. "There's still time."

"Totally." Claire rested her hand on Dylan's shoulder. "We can come up with a plan for you to kiss him after dinner tonight. That's our specialty." She winked at Massie.

"What I need is a plan to get rid of Olivia." Dylan glared at the perky blonde at the other end of the table. "Plovert is totally into her."

"How do you know?" Massie insisted, even though she knew Dylan was right.

"Last night he asked me to find out if Olivia was into anyone." Dylan smacked her stack of syrupy pancakes with the back of a spoon.

"Oh." Massie slid her compass charm back and forth on the gold chain around her neck.

"Attention, please," Mr. Dingle announced from the front of the room.

Massie was grateful for the interruption. She wanted to make Dylan feel better but had no idea what to tell her. Everyone knew Plovert was into Olivia. He had been stalking her like a hungry bear ever since they'd stepped off the bus.

"Your attention, please." Mr. Dingle pushed his big square glasses up on his nose, then clasped his hands behind his back like he was hiding something back there. "Qui-et!"

The room was silent except for the scraping and clinking of knives and forks against china plates.

Once he had everyone's attention, Mr. Dingle revealed what he had been concealing. Everyone burst into hysterical laughter when he held up a tree branch with a pair of satin underwear dangling from it.

"I found this hanging from a tree at the beginning of Honeysuckle Trail behind the girls' cabin," he said. "And the worst part is, it was hanging a few feet away from an innocent snowy owl's nest."

The room exploded into more laughter. Claire turned bright red and looked at Layne. But Layne didn't notice. Her face was buried inside her backpack. She was pretending to search for something of great importance.

"Not only is dyed satin a huge environmental hazard . . ." Mr. Dingle took off his glasses. His beady eyes searched the crowd. "But I'd hoped a few days in the wilderness would have taught you to respect nature." He waved the stick and underwear around like a shredded battle flag. "I demand to know who is responsible."

The room was silent, except for a few false accusations from the boys' table.

"If no one comes forward, you will all pay." Mr. Dingle put his glasses back on and pushed them into position with his index finger. "How does a six-mile hike and no lunch sound?"

The murmurs built until everyone was speaking at full volume.

"Claire, isn't that *your* underwear?" Alexandra shouted from the other girls' table. "You have, like, ten pairs of those."

"She'sright," Carrie said. "She'stheonlyone who wears fullpanties. Weallwearthongs."

The boys cracked up and started punching Cam. He turned bright red and whacked them back.

Claire hunched over and rubbed her forehead.

Massie glared at Layne, silently threatening her to speak up, or else.

"Uh, I know who did it," Layne offered softly.

"Louder," Massie said through her teeth.

Claire looked at Layne with a worried look on her face. She obviously didn't want her friend going down like this.

Layne already took enough heat for her crazy outfits and disgusting food obsessions. If everyone found out she'd hidden dirty underwear in a tree, she'd never recover. It would be the final nail in her social coffin.

"I know who did it." Claire jumped to her feet.

The room was silent. Massie's heart was pounding. She couldn't bring herself to look at Claire, even though she was dying to see what would happen next.

"They're *hers*." Claire pointed at Alicia.

"What?" Alicia screeched. She slapped her hand against her chest. "What are you tawk-ing about?"

Everyone started whispering.

"Alicia, is this true?" Mr. Dingle asked.

"No," Alicia insisted. Her cheeks turned the color of Claire's grape juice. "'Course not."

"Because if you're lying, everyone in this room is looking at a six-mile hike and—"

"It's true," Livvy piped up. "I saw Claire lend her a pair when we got here."

"I saw that too," Alexandra said.

"Me too," Layne shouted. When no one was looking she mouthed "Thank you" to Claire.

"Ew, why would I ever borrow Claire's underwear?" Alicia shouted. "I think I can afford my own."

"You borrowed it, remember?" Olivia was obviously trying to be helpful. "It was the day we got here. We were unpacking and Claire gave you—"

Alicia elbowed Olivia in the stomach.

"Ow," Olivia wailed. "What'd you do that for?"

Alicia glared at Olivia until she finally realized she had made matters worse for her friend. "Ehmagawd, I am soooo sorry," she whispered.

Massie was too shocked to get involved. She could not believe Claire had the guts to blame Alicia. But then again, Alicia kind of deserved it for putting the moves on Cam. But hadn't Alicia just been paying Claire back for kissing Josh? The situation was too complicated to pick a side, even for Massie. She popped a home fry in her mouth and crossed her legs. It was nice to watch someone else's social life crash and burn for a change.

It wasn't long before the boys started chanting, "Alicia Rivera's underwear-a," over and over again.

"It's not mine." Alicia jumped to her feet.

But no one heard her over the chanting.

"Thanks ah-lot!" Alicia shouted at Claire before she turned and bolted. It was the first time Massie had ever seen her run.

"Come back here, Ms. Rivera," Mr. Dingle insisted. But Alicia ran past him and straight out the door.

"I better go see if she's okay." Olivia threw her napkin on the table and chased after her friend.

"Me too." Dylan stuffed two bagels and a few slices of cheese in the pockets of her bomber jacket. "They're for Kristen," she said when she noticed Massie's look of disgust. "It's my turn to bring her food."

Massie grinned. She felt light and utterly stress-free, like she was on a spa vacation. This was so not her problem.

The chanting got louder.

"ALICIA RIVERA'S UNDERWEAR-A!

"ALICIA RIVERA'S UNDERWEAR-A!

"ALICIA RIVERA'S UNDERWEAR-A!

"ALICIA RIVERA'S UNDERWEAR-A!"

"That's enough!" Mr. Dingle shouted. He dropped the stick and the dirty underwear in the trash. The chanting turned into whispers and then finally faded away.

"I feel terrible," Claire announced softly.

"Explain." Massie took a sip of orange juice and popped another home fry in her mouth. She felt like she was watching a movie. She understood perfectly why Claire felt guilty blaming an innocent girl, but she didn't want the show to end. Why put out a perfectly good fire when you can throw more fuel on it and watch it burn?

"I know for a fact that was Layne's doing, not Alicia's," Claire whispered. "I was just so mad at her for trying to kiss Cam."

Massie tore off a piece of baguette and dipped it in the raspberry jelly jar.

"I have to go say I'm sorry," Claire insisted.

"Tell me why you feel that way." Massie imitated the shrink she had to see when she was having night terrors.

"I just do." Claire stepped over the bench, grabbed her baby blue puffy coat, and made a dash for the exit.

Massie turned back to the table. Layne was staring at her blankly.

"Nice going, Layne . . . the Stain." Massie lifted her eyebrows and half smiled.

Layne pushed back her chair and ran after Claire.

Massie turned to her left, then her right, looking for someone to crack up with. But no one was there. "Coming," she shouted to no one in particular. Then she ran out of the dining pavilion before anyone realized she had been left behind.

She expected to see the girls fighting outside the door but the campsite was strangely peaceful. The wind had died down, taking the bite out of the cold air. Now it just felt clean and refreshing. Massie felt the weight of sadness inside her body when she realized it was their last day at Forever Wild campsite. It had turned out to be one of the best weeks ever . . . for her.

The shower house seemed like a logical place to start looking for her friends, because girls in tears usually ran to the nearest sink. But the high-pitched shriek coming from inside the girls' cabin told her otherwise.

"I hate you!" she heard Dylan shout.

Massie picked up speed. She couldn't stand to miss another second. She ran up the porch steps, two at a time. "What's going on?" she asked as she threw open the door.

The warm spicy smell of the roaring fire reminded her of her living room when her parents had company. But wait—

who had been using the fireplace? Kristen would never make such a stupid mistake, would she?

It wasn't long before it all made sense. Mr. Myner and Merri-Lee were snuggled together on the couch in front of the fire and Dylan was standing over them with tears rolling down her bright red cheeks. Claire, Layne, Olivia, and Alicia stood behind her with their mouths hanging open. Massie tiptoed over and joined them.

"I am so going to barf up my pancakes," Dylan shouted at them as she rubbed her stomach.

"Pickles, wait." Merri-Lee untangled herself from Mr. Myner and stood up. "You're way off base here."

"You should know," Dylan sneered. "You're ahb-viously an expert on bases."

"Good one," Massie said under her breath. The rest of the girls shook their heads in agreement.

Dylan smiled softly through her tears. Then her expression quickly hardened again. She marched over to Massie's bed and pulled the bagels and cheese out of her pocket. "Here's your stupid breakfast, Kristen." She held the food under the bed until Kristen's hand reached out and grabbed it.

Mr. Myner stood up and smoothed his hands over the front of his Levi's. "Kristen is here?'

"What are you doing?" Massie mouthed to Dylan.

"Like *they* have any right to preach about rules," Dylan sobbed. She stuffed her hands in her coat pockets and ran outside.

"Where is she?" Mr. Myner put his hands on his hips and rested a leg on one of the beanbags.

"Outside." Olivia pointed to the open door. "She just left."

"Not Dylan," Mr. Myner snapped. "Kristen!"

"Oh."

"Hi." Kristen slowly rolled out from under Massie's bed. The back of her short blond hair was matted and tangled. A gray dust bunny was stuck to the back of her neck.

"How long have you been here?' Mr. Myner demanded.

"Coupla days." Kristen's voice trembled as she pushed herself up to stand.

"And you've been living under that bed?"

Massie couldn't tell if he was shocked, angry, or impressed.

Kristen nodded.

"This is turning into a real survival story," Merri-Lee said. "Where's my crew?" She hit a speed dial number on her cell phone and tapped her bare foot while she waited for an answer.

"No cameras," Mr. Myner insisted. He pulled the cell phone out of Merri-Lee's hands and snapped it shut. "This is very serious." He didn't take his eyes off Kristen. "Do your parents know where you are?"

Kristen looked at the fluffy white rug below her feet.

"Kristen!" he shouted.

She jumped but remained silent.

"At the very least, you are facing a suspension for this

stunt," Mr. Myner said. "So you'd better start talking before it gets worse."

"No, please don't," Kristen pleaded. "I only came because I wanted to learn and I couldn't afford the fifteen hundred dollars."

"Oh, this story is good enough to drive Oprah to binge eat." Merri-Lee turned to Mr. Myner and pressed her palms together like she was about to start praying. "Please, let me get my crew."

A look of utter disgust washed over his face. "I refuse to dignify that request with a response."

Merri-Lee smiled flirtatiously and tickled him under his ribs. "Isn't *that* a response?" She giggled at her own cleverness.

Mr. Myner batted her hand away and turned to Kristen. "What you did was wrong on so many levels—"

"Please, Mr. Myner." Kristen started crying openly. "If I get suspended, I'll lose my scholarship and my parents will—"

"You should have thought of that before." He unclipped his cell phone from the side of his Levi's. "Principal Burns," he said, and the phone dialed her number automatically.

"This is so unfair!" Kristen pushed past Mr. Myner and ran out the door.

Mr. Myner snapped his phone shut. "Get back here, Ms. Gregory."

"I'll get her." Massie raced after her friend without a second thought.

"No, you won't," Mr. Myner barked. "Get back here."

"Massie, come back," Claire shouted. "You're gonna get in trouble."

"That's right—she is," Mr. Myner confirmed. "Big trouble."

"I'll get her." Claire hurried outside.

"Oh puh-lease," Alicia hollered. "Like they'll ever listen to *you*. Don't worry, Mr. Myner, I'll find them. They'll listen to *me* way before they'll ever listen to Kuh-laire. Be right back."

Massie leaned up against her birch tree and waited for Claire and Alicia to catch up. But Alicia didn't see her and was screaming, "Massie, stop! Massie, stop!" over and over again until she and Claire found Massie behind the cabin.

"Hurry." Massie wasn't sure what her plan was. All she knew was that her best friends needed her help.

"We have to go back," Claire panted. "Or Mr. Myner will kill us."

"Do what you want, but I'm not going to abandon my friends in their time of need," Massie said.

"Given." Alicia smirked.

Claire started chewing on her thumbnail and looked back at the cabin.

"Dylan? Kristen?" Massie shouted toward the forbidden trails that were a few feet away. "Are you back there?"

"Massie?" Dylan whisper-yelled. "Is this a trap?"

"No, this isn't a trap. Puh-lease!" Massie looked genuinely offended by the suggestion.

"Who's with you?" Kristen called.

"It's me, Alicia, and maybe Claire," Massie said. "If she doesn't run back to Mr. Myner."

Claire took her nail out of her mouth and folded her arms across her chest. She was in.

"Tell me where you are," Massie snapped. "Before he finds us."

"Bear Claw Trail," Kristen said.

"We're on our way."

"Wait." Claire gripped Massie by the shoulder. "If we go back there unsupervised, we'll get expelled. Mr. Myner told us that on the first day, remember?"

Massie glared at her. "What's he gonna do? Expel *all* of us? Puh-lease. We're the most popular girls in the entire grade. The school would be so lame without us and he totally knows that."

"I know but—"

"Just leave, then," Alicia snapped. "No one wants you here anyway."

Claire gave Alicia the dirtiest look she possibly could. Then she pushed through them and led the way up Bear Claw Trail.

Kristen and Dylan were sitting together on a fallen log a few yards away. Both of their faces were streaked with mascara and eyeliner. Massie wanted to make fun of them but decided it was probably better to wait.

"Pickles," Merri-Lee called from the head of the trail.

"Gir-rls?" Mr. Myner joined in. "Let's talk about this."

"Hurry," Kristen mouthed. "This way."

"How do *you* know?" Massie whispered.

"I memorized the trail maps." Kristen touched her index finger to her lips then signaled for them to hurry.

They followed Kristen deep into the woods for what seemed like twenty minutes without saying a word. Finally, they stopped to give Alicia a chance to catch up. She was holding her boobs to keep them from bouncing as she hurried toward them.

"Where are we?" Alicia looked around. "The trail ended ages ago."

Tall bare trees surrounded them on all sides. Even though they had no leaves, they still managed to block the sky. The ground was covered in fallen branches, dead leaves, and patches of thick moss that reminded Massie of the putting green at OCD. She felt insulated by nature. On one hand it felt cozy and cocoonlike and on the other it felt like she was in a coffin, about to be buried alive.

"Uh." Kristen ran her fingers through her short blond hair.

"Whaddaya mean, *uhhhh*?" Alicia asked.

"Just give me a minute." Kristen held up a finger. "I can totally figure this out."

"You better." Dylan's voice was a flat monotone, like a robot's. "Because there is something behind that tree with big black eyes and it's looking right at us."

Massie felt her heart drop before she even saw what Dylan was talking about.

"Nobody move," Kristen whispered. "That will only make it charge us."

"What is it?" Massie heard herself ask. Her voice sounded distant and strange, like it belonged to someone else, someone who was about to die.

"I believe the Latin term is *Ursus arctos*," Kristen murmured.

"And in English?" Dylan snapped.

"Grizzly bear," Claire gasped for Kristen.

"Ehmagawd, what do we do?" Alicia grabbed Claire's arm, then immediately let go when she realized what she had done.

"Crouch down and pretend you're a small nonthreatening rodent," Kristen said softly.

"What?" Dylan snapped.

"Shhhhh," everyone seemed to hiss.

"Just do it." Kristen lowered herself into a squat. She held out her hands and curled her fingers so they looked like tiny squirrel claws. "I read it in your survival guide."

The girls couldn't argue with her, since none of them had bothered to read the thick handout. In fact, Massie remembered using it to blot her lip gloss minutes before she met up with Derrington.

One by one they crouched down. Massie squeezed her eyes shut, made tiny claws with her hands, and thanked Gawd she would die knowing what it was like to kiss a boy.

"No one has any food with them, right?" Kristen whispered.

The girls were squatting like squirrels, trying to outsmart the beast that was glaring at them from behind the trees.

"I wish," Dylan whispered back. "If I'd known we were going to spend the rest of our lives lost in the Adirondacks, I would have finished my pancakes."

"Shhhh," Massie insisted, near tears.

Claire discreetly stuck her index finger in her puffy jacket pocket. She wrapped her fist around the half-eaten bag of gummies and sours Cam had given her to keep them away from the hungry animal that was closing in on her. Hopefully, when their mangled bodies were discovered, someone would find the candy in her hand. It would be a detail the press would find sad and charming. Cam would read the article and know that he had been with Claire during her final hours. If only she could offer the same comfort to her family. The thought of her parents crying broke her heart. But the idea of Todd taking her room, after she'd finally gotten to decorate it her own way, filled Claire with enough rage to face the predator head on. If she could stand up to the Pretty Committee, surely she could take on a wild animal.

Claire slowly lifted the bag out of her pocket, hiding it from Dylan, who had been whining about her hunger pains for the last half hour. There was no way she'd be able to untie the knot with one finger, so she poked a hole through the bag instead, dragged a sour toward the opening, and held it in her palm. Everyone was praying with their eyes closed, so they didn't see Claire throw the candy. She tossed it on purpose to the far left of the animal so it would follow the food and leave them alone. But the sour hit a tree and never made it anywhere near its intended target.

"Ehmagawd, did you hear that?" Dylan opened her eyes. "Someone is shooting at us!"

"No one is shooting," Kristen whispered. "It was probably just a falling acorn."

"Are you sure?"

"Totally."

They closed their eyes and continued praying.

Claire went through the entire poke, drag, and drop process again. Only this time she took two pieces instead of one, in case she missed again.

The second toss was even more pathetic than the first. Claire had no clue where it landed.

"This one is for love," Claire told herself as she drew back her arm for the third time. She pictured Cam dressed as Camille and remembered him leaning in to give her a kiss. The memory filled her with strength and determination. This time she threw with more power than she knew she had.

Suddenly, the beast tore off as if a land mine had exploded an inch away from its paws.

"It's gone," Claire announced.

"Ehmagawd, what *was* that?" Alicia opened her big brown eyes.

"It looked like Bambi," Kristen cooed. "I think it was a baby fawn."

"Aren't they vegetarians?" Claire asked.

No one answered.

Claire desperately wanted to tell them how she'd saved their lives, but then they'd know she had sours and gummies. And sharing them was out of the question.

"It was Gawd," Massie declared. "I totally prayed and it worked."

"Nice going." Alicia patted Massie on the back.

"Well, whatever it was, it was our only hope for a decent meal." Dylan stood up and brushed the dried crushed leaves off her knees.

"You sound like Brian from *Hatchet*," Massie said.

"Who?"

"I think he's one of the nonsoccer guys on our trip." Alicia twisted her hair into a knot on the top of her head and stuck a twig through the center to keep it in place.

"Oh, right." Dylan considered this, then paused. "But wait, if he goes to Hatchet, what's he doing on an OCD-Briarwood field trip?"

"No." Massie rolled her eyes. "Brian is the character in that book *Hatchet* Mr. Myner has been reading to us."

"Oh, I love that novel." Kristen beamed. "I read it, like, four years ago . . ." Her voice trailed off. "Maybe I'll memorize it."

"Well, did it mention how to get unlost?"

"I don't remember." Kristen was back in navigation mode. "This way." She pointed to the right and started clomping though the dense forest. The rest of the girls followed. They had no choice. Kristen was the only one who'd taken any interest in the trail maps over the last few days.

"Why hasn't anyone sent help?" Dylan whined.

"Seriously," Kristen agreed. "You'd think your mother would be out here with a team of celebrity rescue dogs."

"Puh-lease, she's way too busy snuggling with Mr. Myner." Dylan looked beyond disgusted, as though she had just been forced to lick white deodorant chunks from the geography teacher's hairy pits.

"Well, we're going to freeze to death if someone doesn't rescue us soon." Claire breathed warm air onto her frozen fingers.

"The memory of cuddling up with Cam last night is keeping *me* warm," Alicia said.

Claire felt her spine stiffen and stopped moving. She glared into Alicia's eyes, silently asking, "You did not just go there, did you?"

Alicia responded by biting her bottom lip and nodding slowly.

"Why did you two stop walking?" Massie called over her shoulder.

"We have to keep moving east if we're ever going to find our way out of here. It looks like we're losing light," Kristen added.

Claire and Alicia ignored them and continued staring into each other's eyes.

"Oh yeah?" Claire wanted to stop herself from saying what she was about to say, but it was too late. Common sense was no longer the gatekeeper of her words: anger was. "Well, I have the memory of kissing Josh *and* Cam to keep *me* warm."

Everyone stopped.

"Really?" Alicia folded her arms across her chest and shifted her weight to one leg. "Well, at least I have hair on my forehead to keep *me* warm."

Claire resisted the urge to tug on her short blond bangs.

"That's just great, because I haaaave . . ." Claire stalled while she searched for something bad to say about Alicia's looks. But it wasn't easy. "I have . . . I have room in my *sweater* to keep *me* warm."

"Well, you won't have room in those Gap jeans if you keep eating those sours when you think we're not looking." Alicia looked at Dylan when she said that.

Claire's body shook with rage.

"You have food?" Dylan was too excited to be resentful.

"Hand it over." Massie held out her palm.

Claire reached into her pocket and pulled out the bag. She felt a pinch behind her eyes and begged herself not to cry. They would think it was because she was giving up her secret food stash, but that wasn't it at all. Claire didn't want them trivializing Cam's gift by calling it food. The gummies and sours were so much more than that. They were love tokens—*her* love tokens.

Massie stuck her open hand under Claire's nose. Claire slapped the bag in Massie's palm and looked away.

"Seriously, Claire." Kristen sounded disappointed. "How would you like it if I led myself out of here and left you all in the dirt to die?" She dug her hand into the open bag Massie passed around.

"I'd love to see that." Dylan chomped down on a green gummy.

"See what?"

"See you find your way out of here." Dylan chewed. "Because I think you're just as clueless as we are."

"Really?" Kristen took a step toward Dylan and pointed a finger in her face. "Then *you* lead." She sat down on a fallen log and crossed her legs.

"No way," Alicia pleaded. "Dyl, I love you to death but you can't get us out of here. You don't even know which way *east* is."

"No one does." Massie twirled her necklace around her finger.

"You do," Claire said softly.

"Huh?" Massie looked annoyed.

"You know which way east is."

Massie put her hands on her hips. "What's that supposed to mean?"

"It means you have a compass around your neck." Claire pointed at the gold chain Massie had been tugging on all morning.

"What?" Massie looked down. "Oh yeah." She giggled.

Claire wanted to remind everyone it was the third time she had saved them, but it was too late. The girls were already hugging Massie and jumping up and down, calling *her* their hero.

"Okay, okay." She pushed them away. "Let's not break it." Massie pulled the necklace over her head and closed her palm around it.

"Lemme see it." Kristen was obviously anxious to see if she had been leading them in the right direction.

"Not until everyone makes up." Massie held her closed fist behind her back.

Everyone's smiles quickly faded.

"Go on." Massie pointed her chin at Dylan. "Why don't you start?"

"Why me?"

"Because you were the one who ran out here in the first place."

"Yeah, well, no one told you to follow me."

"Fine." Massie smirked. "Then I'll start. I'm sorry I followed you out here. I really, really am. Be-lieve me."

Everyone giggled. Even Dylan cracked a smile.

"Dylan, I'm sorry I said you didn't know which way east was," Alicia offered. "I'm sure you do."

"Forgiven." Dylan waved her away like it had been no big deal.

"Now can I please check the compass?" Kristen said

"Not yet." Massie looked at Claire and Alicia.

Alicia turned away.

"Kuh-laire." Massie folded her arms across her chest and tapped her foot impatiently.

"Fine." Claire knew Massie was right. It was time to end this feud and she certainly had a lot to apologize for, so why not go first? At least if they died out here, she'd go with a clean conscience.

"Alicia, I'm sorry I kissed Josh, but I honestly thought you said you were over him." Alicia didn't say anything, so Claire continued. "And I only did it because I was upset about Cam liking Nina. I was never trying to steal him away from you. I swear."

"Why didn't you just tell me? I spent all week acting like a total LBR trying to figure out who he liked."

"I guess I was scared you'd be mad." Claire lifted her eyes to meet Alicia's, even though she was deathly afraid of what she might see in them. "Or that you'd try to get back at me."

"Puh-lease, that's so unlike me." Alicia batted her eyelashes with exaggerated innocence.

Claire looked to the others, hoping for a little backup. Everyone looked away. "Is it really so unlike you to seek revenge?"

Alicia giggled nervously. Her cheeks turned bright red.

Claire could tell she was making Alicia uncomfortable. It felt too good to stop. "I would have gladly told you about Josh if I thought for one second you'd try to understand. But that's not something you like to do, is it? You'd much rather plan and plot and—"

"That's enough." Alicia held her palm in front of Claire's face. "What did you expect me to do, Kuh-laire? Thank you for stabbing me in the back? Hand you your knife back in case you ever wanted to use it again?"

Alicia was totally right. Claire had betrayed her friend and had been more concerned with the punishment than the crime. Was it because it seemed impossible to imagine the beautiful and popular Alicia as a victim? Or had Claire been too busy thinking about her own feelings to even try? Either way, she knew she had been wrong.

"I'm really, really sorry, Alicia. I didn't mean to hurt you." The puddle of tears in Claire's eyes proved that this time she actually meant what she said, and for all the right reasons.

"It's okay." Alicia's voice was forgiving. "I'm sorry for using Cam to get back at you."

"Friends?" Claire looked up. She held out her arms.

"No way," Alicia snapped. "Not after that underwear thing you pulled."

Claire had forgotten all about *that.*

"Alicia Rivera's underwear-a," Dylan chanted.

"It's not funny!" Alicia stomped her foot.

"It kind of is." Massie covered her mouth.

Everyone laughed except Alicia. But the tops of her lips curled up like she wanted to.

"You have to promise to tell everyone it wasn't mine," Alicia insisted.

"Promise."

"Then forgiven." Alicia smiled.

"Thanks." Claire smiled back.

"World peace?" Massie lifted her little fingers. The girls gathered around her and stood in a tight circle, linked by their pinkies.

"World peace," they echoed.

"Can I see that compass now?'" Kristen was bouncing up and down on her toes.

"Yup." Massie handed it to her.

Kristen examined the needle, then tilted the round face from side to side. "Oops," she said under her breath. She turned her body to the left. "Everyone ready?"

"Were you trying to get us lost on purpose so you wouldn't have to go back?" Dylan asked.

"I may be scared of my parents, but I'm more afraid of starving to death," Kristen said.

"Don't worry," Alicia assured them. "My father will fix all of this."

"So will mine," Massie offered.

"Mine too," Claire lied. The only thing her father could do was cheer them up by doing a funny dance or singing with a mouthful of Double-Stuf Oreos.

"Great, then off we go." Kristen wiped her eyes and led them back the way they'd come.

"Look, high-heel prints." Alicia pointed to the soft ground. "Dylan, do you think your mother is out here looking for us?"

"Those are deer tracks." Kristen rolled her eyes.

"People eat deer, you know." Dylan perked up.

"I'd rather eat my arm than eat a cute little deer." Massie held her hand to her heart.

"I wouldn't mind eating your arm either," Dylan said.

"What?" Alicia giggled.

"It's true," Dylan said. "If I had to eat one of us for survival, I'd pick Massie."

"Thanks." Massie smiled with pride.

"Why her?" Kristen sounded offended.

"Because there's no fat on her but she's not too skinny either," Dylan explained. "She'd be like a quail or a small chicken."

"What's wrong with me?" Kristen whined.

"A little too muscular." Dylan quickly dismissed her absurd suggestion. "You'd be too gamey."

"Fine with me," Kristen said. "It's not like I want to be cooked."

"Sounds like you do," Massie teased.

"And Claire." Dylan tapped her temple. "You'd make a nice little dessert."

"Thanks." Claire wasn't sure if she had just been complimented or not, but she was grateful to have been included.

"Hey, doesn't anyone like breast meat?" Alicia opened her jacket and flashed her tight-fitting sweater.

They all burst out laughing.

"Ehmagawd, I'm so going to pee in my pants." Alicia doubled over and held her bladder.

"Just squat," Kristen suggested.

"Ew, no way." Alicia rolled her eyes.

"Pee in your pants," Dylan suggested. "They'll dry."

"You're disgusting." Massie playfully slapped her friend on the arm.

"Maybe." Dylan smiled. "But at least I'm warm." She lifted her long, olive green DKNY cardigan and revealed a massive wet spot around her crotch.

"Ew!" They shouted and took off; even Alicia ran away.

"Come back and give me a hug." Dylan stretched out her arms and chased after them. The louder they screamed, the harder she laughed. "You can't escape the pee-pee monster!" she shouted over and over again. "Urine trouble! Get back here."

The girls ran as fast as they could. They were choking on their laughter and tripping over each other as Dylan chased them right out of the woods.

All of a sudden they were back in camp, not even knowing how they'd gotten there.

"Urine for it!" Dylan shouted from a few feet behind them. She had no idea her victims were now standing by the fire pit while Mr. Myner stared at them in disgust.

He kept his eyes on them as he spoke into his walkie-talkie. "I have a twenty on the missing girls, over."

"Are they all safe and accounted for? Over," the voice said back.

Mr. Myner was about to answer when Dylan shot out of the woods. She was running on her toes, her arms stretched out over her head and her legs splayed out to the sides like she was doing the funky chicken dance.

"Come give the pee-pee monster a big hug," she shouted. She stopped the second she realized everyone was staring at her.

Kristen's phlegmy laugh was the only sound anyone heard after that.

Finally, after a long, uncomfortable stare-down, Mr. Myner broke the silence. "Do you have any idea how many people have been looking for you?"

"Pickles." Merri-Lee hugged her daughter as hard as she possibly could.

"Ew," Alicia said under her breath.

The girls lost it at the thought of Merri-Lee pressed up against the pee-pee monster.

"Where's my crew?" She pulled away from her daughter and looked around the campsite. "Why wasn't anyone shooting our reunion?"

"Are you okay?" Cam rushed over to Claire.

"Yeah." Claire relaxed her eyelids, trying to look weak and forlorn.

A group of girls surrounded Massie until Derrington

arrived. Then they stepped back to give the happy couple some private time to reconnect.

"Girls, hurry to the dining pavilion and get some food before it's all cleared away," Mr. Myner ordered.

"Awesome, you're the best!" Dylan blurted out, temporarily forgetting the grudge she had been holding against him.

The other girls hugged Mr. Myner and thanked him endlessly for his compassion.

"Please meet me in my quarters in twenty minutes," he said, refusing to hug them back. His stiff, stoic posture reminded Claire of the tall trees that had been staring down at them all morning.

"You got it," Massie shouted.

The girls raced toward the dining pavilion, salivating for whatever scraps they could salvage from lunch.

"Maybe it's a good thing he's in love with my mother," Dylan said.

"I know," Alicia agreed. "He's so going to let us off the hook."

"I bet if you start calling him Dad, he'll forget the whole thing ever happened." Massie giggled.

Claire laughed too, knowing the worst was behind her. She'd kissed Cam, made up with Alicia, and was finally out of the woods.

Or so it seemed.

```
┌─────────────────────────────────────────────┐
│          LAKE PLACID, NEW YORK                │
│          FOREVER WILD CAMPSITE                │
│          MR. MYNER'S QUARTERS                 │
│          Wednesday, February 25th             │
│                 2:11 P.M.                     │
└─────────────────────────────────────────────┘
```

"Kill me now." Dylan found her mother's green-and-yellow silk twill Hermès pocket scarf behind the leather pillow on Mr. Myner's couch.

"Ew." Alicia winced when she saw it.

Massie found more than Merri-Lee's scarf unsettling. It was creepy in general being in Mr. Myner's quarters. It smelled like a combination of Irish Spring soap and burnt coffee.

Behind them, in the center of the room, was his four-post bed. It was half-made. His navy-and-red plaid comforter had been haphazardly pulled up but had not been smoothed out or tucked in. And the pillows still had dents in their centers from where his big head and thick hair must have lain all night. *Ew!* Even though he was better looking than most teachers, the image of him sleeping was borderline repulsive. Did he drool? Snore? Have brutal morning breath? Massie shook those thoughts away as quickly as they'd come. She longed for the powdery, perfumey fragrance of the girls' cabin.

"Do you really think he's outside calling our parents?" Kristen sniffled.

"I know he's been in close contact with Dylan's." Massie couldn't help herself.

"Shut up." Dylan whipped the scarf at Massie's face.

Claire twisted the empty candy bag around her hand. Her fingers started turning different shades of purple and Massie looked away.

"Can I use that?" Kristen sniffled and reached for Merri-Lee's scarf. Massie handed it to her without a second thought.

"Relax, Kristen." Dylan rubbed her friend on the back. "We are not going to get into any trouble. He's just trying to teach us a lesson."

Kristen dabbed her eyes. "So you don't think he's really calling anyone?"

"I bet he is," Alicia speculated. "But my parents will blame *him*, not me. He lost *us*. Remember that."

Kristen burst into tears. "Yeah, but I wasn't even supposed to *be* here. My mom thinks I'm at a soccer match."

The five girls crossed their legs and sat up straight when they heard Mr. Myner clomping up the steps outside his quarters.

"Shhhh." Massie leaned across the couch and slapped Kristen on the thigh. "Dylan's dad is coming."

"Daaaaad," Dylan burped.

The girls were cracking up when he walked in.

"That's good, ladies, get it all out." He closed the door behind him. "Because you may never laugh again."

He poured himself a cup of coffee from the black cappuccino maker on top of his mini-fridge. Then he lifted the brown ceramic mug to his nose and savored the aroma like he was in a Maxwell House commercial. For a minute Massie wondered if he'd forgotten they were there. His casual demeanor was starting to make her nervous.

Mr. Myner set the mug on the mantel, unlaced his hiking boots, and set them neatly by the door. The steam from his coffee rose in ribbons and swirls, floated away, and vanished. It had no idea how lucky it was.

Finally, he hooked his palm through the handle of his mug and settled into the tan leather club chair by the fireplace. After a loud, slurpy sip, Mr. Myner uncrossed his legs and angled his body toward the girls on the couch.

"What you did today was very dangerous," he began, sounding like a concerned father. He wasn't mad, just worried. Massie felt the tension in her shoulders melt away. The worst was over.

"But what also concerns me is how long it took you to find your way back to camp." His eyes narrowed and the muscles on the sides of his jaw pulsated. "To think that we've spent the past three days learning how to navigate in the wilderness, and you lost your way on a marked trail." He wiped his brow with his hand. "It sickens me."

Massie raised her hand. "I think we would have had an easier time getting back if you hadn't taken our cell phones and two-ways." She looked at the others for reinforcement.

They nodded their heads in agreement. "I mean, we totally would have called—we just couldn't."

"The idea, Ms. Block, was to teach you how to survive without these things," he spat. "Which just furthers my point. The whole lesson was completely lost on you."

"I studied the map trails," Kristen offered. "I knew we had to go east."

"Then why did it take you five hours to find us?" Mr. Myner ran his hand through his hair. "If you'd gone east, it would have taken you five minutes." He paused. "And what exactly are you doing on this trip *anyway*?"

Kristen dabbed her eyes with the Hermès scarf.

"I warned you about the consequences if any of you took off into the woods, did I not?"

No one said a word.

"If anything had happened to you girls, OCD would have been faced with so many lawsuits, the school would have had to close its doors forever."

"Good thing we're okay." Massie tried to sound positive. "Right?"

"Yes, Massie." Mr. Myner's voice sounded strained, like he was doing his best not to snap. "But I'm afraid you are still going to pay the price for breaking the rules. After all, we have to set an example for the other students. So, I have spoken to Principal Burns and she agrees." He took a deep breath. "All of you have officially been expelled from OCD, effective immediately."

The girls gasped. They'd expected a lecture on responsibility and maybe a detention. But *this*? No one knew how to respond.

"You mean suspended?" Massie felt queasy. His words floated right above her skin, unable to fully penetrate.

"No, I mean expelled."

"Uh, don't you think that's a little harsh?" Massie asked, her insides churning. "Our parents will never go for that."

"They have already been notified," Mr. Myner shot back. "We have arranged for a bus to take you home this afternoon. They will be waiting for you when it arrives."

Dylan stood up and put her hands on her hips. "If I hadn't been so traumatized by you and my mother, I never would have run off in the first place." She glared at him. "Did you tell *that* to Principal Burns? Did you tell her I was traumatized? Or did that slip your mind?"

"Your mother is not on the faculty and we are both adults," Mr. Myner replied evenly. "We have every right to keep company."

"Well, she'll be dumping you now," Dylan said under her breath as she sat down.

"My father is so going to fight this," Alicia said, trying to sound like she wasn't scared. "He is going to sue you for losing us, OCD for expelling us, and the Adirondacks for not making better trails."

"And for discriminating against the poor," Kristen added.

"The poor?" Mr. Myner shook his head in confusion.

"Yeah," Kristen sobbed. "If I weren't poor, I wouldn't have had to sneak up here and then I never would have gotten caught and I never would have run away and—"

Mr. Myner lifted his palm. "That's enough. The bus will be here in thirty-five minutes, so you'd better hurry back to the cabin and gather your things."

"What about all of the stuff you stole from us when we got here?" Massie asked.

"It will all be on the bus."

"Sorry," Claire squeaked. It was the first time she'd spoken since he entered the room.

"So am I," Mr. Myner said. "There's nothing more upsetting than a wasted education."

Massie stood up and the rest of the girls followed. She was too shocked to accept the idea that she would no longer be going to OCD. There had to be something her parents could do, right? She had gotten herself out of worse situations in the past—how hard could this be? These questions would have to be answered later. Right now her insides felt heavy and tired, like they did after a major crying session. And her brain felt slow and numb. Yes, later.

Mr. Myner held the door open for the girls. One by one they filed past him and stepped back out into the cold. Everyone was standing on his porch steps, waiting to see if they were okay. Even the nonsoccer guys looked concerned. If it hadn't been for the dirty clothes, the matted hair, and the ruined future, Massie would have felt like a total A-lister stepping out of the revolving door at the Ritz-Carlton.

"What happened?" Derrington handed her a fistful of wildflowers. They were a little brown and crispy from the dry winter air but the gesture was a total ten.

Massie took the flowers and sniffed them. One of the sharp leaves poked her lip and she fondly remembered Doose and his stiff whiskers. She had come such a long way in the past three days. And now this.

"We've been expelled," Massie announced to her public.

"What?" Derrington's voice cracked. "You're joking, right?"

He quickly realized she wasn't when he saw Kristen's purple face and swollen eyes.

"Hey, what's she doing here?" someone shouted.

Seconds later, the girls were enveloped by sympathetic hugs and words of encouragement and solidarity.

"Let'sgoontrike," Carrie shouted.

"Yeah!" everyone shouted.

"They will not get away with this." Layne punched the air.

Massie felt better than she had all day. She loved how everyone was uniting on her behalf. "Fight the power!"

"Fight the power!" they responded.

Massie looked for her friends, hoping they were feeling as invigorated as she was. But they had their own ways of dealing.

Claire was off to the side of the group with Cam. He was wiping her cheeks with his thumb. Dylan was shouting at her mother, begging her to do something. Kristen was banging on

Mr. Myner's door, pleading with him to reconsider, and Alicia and Olivia were hugging Josh and Plovert goodbye. Mr. Myner finally opened the door. Kristen fell to the ground and grabbed his legs.

"Please, take it back," she begged. "I'll do anything. I'll memorize the entire globe if you want. Even the latitudes and longitudes. *Everything.*"

"Get up, Ms. Gregory." His tone was cold and measured. "You now have twenty-three minutes to collect your things."

"Tree hugger!" Kristen shouted at him. She wiped the snot away from her nose and ran off to the cabin.

"Girls, the bus is waiting!" Mr. Myner said. "Go!"

Massie took one last look around.

It was the last time she'd ever see these faces again.

"*Bass Ackwards and Belly Up* is a new novel I just read and ah-dored. It's about four BFFs who, for a juicy reason I won't divulge, decide to not go to college to pursue their dreams. It's one of those things most of us fantasize about but don't have the guts to do. Maybe that's why I loved it, for the vicarious thrill. Or maybe because I was dying to know if they'd succeed."

— **Lisi Harrison**, author of the #1 *New York Times* bestselling **CLIQUE** series

Harper Waddle, Sophie Bushell, and Kate Foster are about to commit the ultimate suburban sin — bailing on college to pursue their dreams. Middlebury-bound Becca Winsberg is convinced her friends have gone insane...until they remind her she just might have a dream of her own. So what if their lives are bass ackwards and belly up? They'll always have each other.

BASS ACKWARDS AND BELLY UP

AVAILABLE NOW